# Erasure

A.T.H. Webber

ISBN-10: 1477574662
ISBN-13: 978-1477574669

*For Melanie.*

# i.

*I remember, but it is failing. I have strived to erase myself before I go.*

*For as long as I remember her, she can wait for me.*

*For as long as I am remembered, I will have to wait.*

Our world is one that demands recognition. A constant search for reassurance that the individual will be made recognisable by the performance of self, and remembered as one who has been.

At first glance, this might seem to be a phenomenon that is reserved for the age in which we now find ourselves, filled as it is with social media – instantaneous information delivered to our computers and smart-handsets from the brightest, and darkest, recesses of the world.

However, this desire to be remembered has been part of society for thousands of years – beginning when ancient beings enhanced their artistic repertoire from scrawls of what they had hunted that day, to using ground bone and ochre mixed with spit to trace their hands on cave walls next to the childlike scrawls of animals and fish. In essence, changing the message from "this is what can be hunted in the area" to "this is what *I* hunted in this area, and it was *I* that made these marks, for *I* am valuable." This personal appellation might be little more than a mark of authority – a signature that states that the author can be trusted.

But, perhaps it was something more.

Perhaps when we of the 21st century witness these marks made thousands of years ago, we are not just witnessing a shopping list of available local food, we are actually witnessing the moment that human kind recognised their own existence, and with that, their desire to be remembered.

Fast forward to now, to a totally different world. A world that is not only content for a mark to be made, but that the mark must be applauded and scrutinised and compared. Such comparisons are then warped into a nexus of low percentage truths that form a broader narrative in which all participants strive for validation. Unlike our ancient ancestors, whose hands now only depict an anonymous existence in pre-history, the memory of us is maintained with hyper-efficiency by the technology that we use to leave our mark. In short there is little chance of being forgotten with data-stores collating everything we ever do; all while keeping the information fresh and clean.

For centuries there have been those who have believed that there is danger in being remembered, and that being forgotten is a gift that transcends earthly legacy. Taught by those in what is now called 'The Movement', it is a doctrine that follows a two-step process before reaching nirvana. A process that claims that after death the soul moves to a middle plane, watching over those who remember them. Acting as some form of angel or protector until the last person to remember them dies and comes to take their place, the then-forgotten soul being free to move on to the afterlife.

The Movement teaches that this is the reason why those in some religious orders were supposed to remain chaste; their position and earthly sacrifice was to be rewarded by having to wait for only a few years after death before moving to the next world, if indeed there is a new world to move to. No wives, no children, and no real assets to have to pass on – it was as close as a person could get to a clean passport.

More recently, The Movement has fractured, creating factions that seek to promote their particular interpretations of The Movement's manifesto. Some believe themselves to be Messiahs and so seek to do good, intending to be remembered by as many as possible in order to extend their influence and time in the middle ground.

Others seek to do extraordinary harm for the same reasons.

Still others desire to expedite their time in the middle ground by eradicating every last trace of their lives. In this technological age, this is an enterprise that is massive in scope. Bank records, social media, search engine history, GPS, texts, email, and every conceivable permutation of convenience and technology combining to create a far more vivid picture of life than the sharpest of history's photographs.

I was drawn into this para-religious world when She was murdered, and while I am unsure of what is out there in the grey expanse beyond death, I chose this path out of sheer hope.

Hope that we can be together again.

Hope that, even though I do not consider myself religious, there is a chance that The Movement might just be on to something.

If The Movement is wrong in its assumptions and ideals, then at least I have succeeded in holding her memory in pure clarity. If it is right, I hope to see her again and that she welcomes me with love.

She died 40 years ago and, and if I have done what I set out to do, if I have managed to find every trace, I am the last person to remember her.

It has taken many years, and my time draws near. Not because of some angel taking wing, drawing inexorably closer to take me away – I'm just tired, but I have to be sure that what needs to be done has been done, or all this time alone will be for nothing but my selfish desire.

It has been lonely, but I have worked hard toward this goal.

Yes, it is a gamble, but if there is even the slightest chance that I can see Her again…

# 1.

It's sunny, and the day is creeping slowly toward late afternoon, the smell of our sweat is pleasant as it mixes with the summer air. A sweat that comes not from exertion, but quietly leaks through the pores on a day that is just a little too warm.

The kind of sweat that chills the body when the sun sneaks behind a cloud and a breeze whispers over the skin.

Hammock sweat.

Lazing-in-the-backyard sweat.

"It has to be time to open the bar, doesn't it?"

"Mmmm…"

"Honey…wake UP!" she poked me hard in the ribs.

"Ow! Okay, okay. Shit," I said, and laughed, as I extricated myself from the hammock we shared, then rubbed at the string lines that had formed on my arm; red and a perfect stereo of the patterned sling.

"You are aware that violence against loved ones is a sign of addiction…" I told her with mock concern.

"But you knew that! That's what made me fall in love with you – you're an enabler. You don't despise me for my desire for a gin and tonic on a sunny Saturday afternoon." She was staring with a look of faux desperation on her face.

Dear God, I loved her.

"Oh, OH! Just a G & T then? It's a good thing you don't have a more complicated drug of choice."

"Please… I am fading," throwing her hand to her forehead, she fell back into the hammock, giggling.

I turned and left her swinging gently in the yard while I went inside to prepare our afternoon indulgence.

"Try to hang on," I said over my shoulder, "I love you."

"I… I love…you," She said in a voice that sounded like it should have come from one who is lost and baking in some far off desert.

I turned to see that she was now implementing a long-forgotten acting class on death. A performance that would have been distressing if she hadn't been stifling a giggle at the same time.

"Oh the humanity!" I said as I turned to go inside.

"Fuck humanity," she called "I need a G & T!"

*****

With a drink in each hand, I left the kitchen. The tumblers were filled to the brim, and I sipped at them to stop any spilling; a tactic that also meant I could get a head start on the evening's festivities.

The door to the back yard was through the laundry and had a latch that I had been meaning to fix since the previous summer. Placing the drinks on the washing machine, I marvelled that while it hadn't washed clothes in years, it had become a handy ledge to rest things on in order to manipulate the door-latch – an enterprise that involved a deft lift and push of the handle, while applying a judicious bump of the hip to liberate the door from its jamb. I registered that in addition to repairing the

6

latch I should probably paint the door as well – the dirty, peeling paint was probably ten years past its best.

"Next weekend," I said, as I held the door open with my hip, stretching to grab the moisture-beaded plastic tumblers from the machine.

I tottered down the steps, careful to not spill our refreshments, and felt a small sense of triumph upon reaching the flat ground that would allow me to stride purposefully forward, for I was the afternoon's saviour who had brought forth sustenance.

"The bar is O-PEN," I said, stretching out the hand with her drink in it (she liked lime in her gin, while I preferred lemon).

She didn't move.

"Oh, come on, I've only been gone for 10 minutes, you can't have expired … in…"

Something was wrong. It is obvious to me now, but not then. I couldn't register – couldn't process – what was in front of me.

It made no sense that her shirt was so dark, when it should be light blue.

Had she changed clothes?

Why was there a flat dripping noise?

'Phat. Phat… Phat.' Fluid fell from the hammock on to the short-cut grass in thick droplets.

She was just lying there. Looking away from the house.

Then as if someone had hit a switch, I screamed – hard. So hard that for the rest of my days my voice didn't sound like my own, making me wonder if the slight rasp registered to those listening to me that mine was a voice formed by horror, and not a pack-a-day smoking habit.

I held her hand.

I looked for a pulse.

I tried to call out for help, but there was no one to hear my blistered voice.

Fumbling for my phone, I called the emergency number – my fingers that at first were slimy with her blood began sticking to the plastic of the phone as I punched in the numbers.

I didn't know how to broach the enormity of what had happened. When the anonymous person answered in a matter-of-fact tone with "Police, Fire, or Ambulance?" I simply croaked out "Something terrible has happened," and dropped the phone on the ground without disconnecting.

I knelt by her.

I held her hand.

I buried my face in her belly.

I felt the last of her warmth.

I listened to the gentle gurgle of her still settling organs.

I breathed in the smell of her.

Hammock sweat.

Lazing-in-the-backyard sweat.

And blood.

Burying my face even deeper, I sobbed; her stomach absorbing everything my grief produced.

# 2.

I was suspected, of course. I'm not sure I blame them – apart from the fact that I loved her, and had no desire to harm her in any way, I seemed to the investigators to be the obvious choice.

The investigators weren't paid to process love stories. As far as they were concerned, it was another day at the office. An office in which they had to deal with a murder, and sorting it out quickly would allow them to get onto other things – other murders, or whatever else falls within the law-enforcement territory.

The forensic team found a full handprint, blood drying, on the gate that led to the short forested path to the beach. It looked like a macabre stencil of a palm and all five digits. So perfect, it looked as if it had been purposely placed there. All it needed was a signature, and someone would claim it to be the next big thing in urban art.

The investigators did their best to try to implicate me, using every tool they had to try to turn me about in the hope I would give them something they could use. I stuck with the truth, primarily because it was all I had:

I didn't know anyone who would wish to hurt her.

She had no enemies.

She was impossible to be angry with, so how someone would be angry enough to kill her was beyond me.

Even so, the questions kept coming with only slight changes in nuance, a frustrating process of circling back to me as the protagonist in a story they were trying to write. Near breaking point, tired, and frustrated, I decided I was done with it all, "The only way I could have anything to do with her death is if she murdered herself in protest of the way I make a gin and tonic." I said.

"You think this is funny?" the interrogator asked.

"Do I look like I'm enjoying this?" Standing now, I was barely holding it together. "The most important thing in my life has been taken away from me. I love her, I will always love her. Why the FUCK would I want to harm her in any way? Tell me that, and let me go home."

I upended the interview table.

Not something I would usually recommend.

However, as the reinforcements rushed in and pushed me to the floor, I looked at the interrogator and got the feeling that the bruises that were about to be visited on my body would be worth it. It had brought something to the now upturned table that I had been unable to convey with truth and capitulation – my outburst had caused doubt.

\*\*\*\*\*

The autopsy results showed that she was shot in the top of the head, the bullet passing through her skull, pulverising the soft meringue of her brain. The bullet then pushed through the at the boundary where hard and soft palate meet, slashing her tongue, before exiting the soft beautiful flesh underneath her chin only to re-enter her just above the sternum and lodging between her lungs.

She was probably dead when the bullet stopped.

If she wasn't, then it would have been soon after.

The marks around the entry point suggested a silenced weapon, which explained why I hadn't heard it.

I was most likely singing or dancing about the kitchen; it was a perfect day after all. My beautiful girl was outside. We were about to ease into the evening with a stiff drink, then maybe order some pizza from the store in town. We'd play cards until we were too drunk to play by the rules, and so decide to switch to strip poker, which would last a couple of rounds before one of us gave up, stood, and disrobed in order to start the late night session with a hand-guided tour of the other's body.

That was what was supposed to be.

"What do you know about this?" the guy charged with yet another round of interrogation asked, while he opened a laptop and spun it toward me to display a slide show of what I guessed to be the crime scene photographs. I briefly saw a frontal photo of Her, looking like some ghastly Halloween costume-project.

The officer clicked through the files, murmuring an apology by way of "you weren't supposed to see that" while looking for the photo he had been referring to. The images flew by and I felt in turns revolted, and numb. The images were familiar – the house, the backyard, the fence, the hammock. An unusual symbol flashed by and, realising he had passed the image he wanted he clicked back to it.

"I don't know what that is," I said

It was a distinct mark, two circles joined. Drawn in black ink that looked like it came from an indelible pen. Drawn on Her skin.

They asked me again whether I had seen this mark before and I repeated my previous answer.

A knock at the door and it opened, a new face beckoning my captor out in to the hall.

He pulled the door closed behind him, but years of use had rendered the self-closing device a little worse for wear. The door opened again after the officer had let it go, almost in protest to being forced when it would rather close in its own time.

Voices filtered from the corridor.

"I've just got this back from the research geeks," the new voice said "They've found references to marks like this before, although they haven't found any that are this detailed. In other cases it has been drawn on something, somewhere at the scene. This is the first to be found actually drawn on the victim."

"So are we leaning toward this being a potential serial killer then?" asked my interrogator.

"Too early to tell if it is one, or due to the ritualistic nature of symbolism, more than one," replied the newcomer.

"Shit."

*****

After a lengthy court process, in which I felt like nothing more than a passenger, I was acquitted. The case was referred to the police to keep open and I went home.

Not to the beach house, I went home to the city.

# 3.

A couple of months passed, and decided I would put the beach house and everything in it on the market. I wasn't holding much hope for a reasonable price, the market was down and people could barely afford to pay their own mortgages, let alone purchase an additional property. Particularly when that property had had a corpse swinging in a backyard hammock the previous summer.

"Just enjoy it while you have it," said the chirpy sales agent. I just nodded, too tired to talk about what had happened anymore.

I sold our cars, because they reminded me of her - not because I needed the money, we had top-of-the-range life insurance for years...

"If we don't have children, who will look after the remaining one, if one of us dies?" I hated her talking like that, and said if she wanted to go and get insurance, I'd sign but I didn't want to be part of the process. It turns out that she had organised a pretty large insurance policy.

Despite my fire-sale mentality, I still need some kind of transport, so I bought a second-hand car with low miles and a reasonable warranty. I didn't care much for the style of the thing, just that it would get me where I needed to go, should I need to go somewhere. 'Somewhere' being a rare place to visit, as my job allowed me to work from home. Something I had always done; consultancy offers a significant amount of freedom in that respect. In fact, no one at head office, situated on another continent, actually knew what I looked like. I didn't set about making it that way – it's just how things worked out.

The city-house was empty and no amount of working was going to fill it, so I often found myself walking over to the park. It was nearby, and on a good day I could get sufficient wireless reception to do work.

And I didn't care when it dropped out. I'd just stare at things.

However, I wasn't the only one watching things in the park with such interest.

*****

On a day about three months after Her death, I returned home to find my door open.

I looked stupidly at the door latch, trying to make sense of what it meant. It seemed impossible for the door to be open, and yet there it was. Frowning, I looked over my shoulder, then back to the door. I always locked it. A habit ingrained by years of repetition.

I pushed on the door and walked right on into the house. Since she died I didn't feel much threat from anything, I just figured that the worst thing, worse than death, had already happened. Fearless is probably too big a word. Apathy would probably be better suited – I was a solid "meh" on just about everything. All was grey in this new world I inhabited, and nothing seemed to stand out enough to elicit even the slightest emotional flicker.

However, I was almost excited by the prospect of surprising a would-be burglar in my own home.

The idea of contest sent a thrill through me. Eyes wide, I began to look around.

Everything was where it should be. Or, at my best guess, it appeared that way. The place wasn't so neat without Her nagging me to at least try to be a little tidy, so it would take a while to work out if anything had actually been taken.

I rationalised that, perhaps, even though it was inconceivable to me, I hadn't actually locked the door.

I spent so much time walking around in thoughtless stupor that it was possible, but only as a last-resort explanation. In truth, I knew that I had shut the door – pulled on it to hear the silver hasp strike home.

I did that every time.

There didn't appear to be anyone about to leap out at me from some dim and pizza-box laden corner, so my concern ebbed a little. Although, any house has a lot of places for someone to hide if they need to. Perhaps some assailant, surprised that the owner of the place they found themselves in had returned home unexpectedly, was now hidden somewhere, breathing shallowly and waiting for a moment to arise so they could either fight, or run.

"I don't know what's going on here, but coffee will help," I said as I went back to the front door and pushed it closed, listening for the tell-tale click of the lock. Then opened it again. Then closed it. Satisfied with the solid mechanical sound.

I reached into my pocket and pulled out the keys, Her keys, with the little key ring she bought so that hers looked different to mine and we wouldn't take the wrong ones when leaving the house. Something I used to do regularly. It was a problem, She solved it.

For the first time in a very long while I used the deadlock key – the lock had been on the door since we arrived, and was rarely used – but I figured that if there was someone hiding in the place, they were going to have to ask me for a key to get out.

"We're both locked in here now," I said to open space. "If you want coffee you should let me know, and then we can discuss how you can get the fuck out of my house."

No one answered.

# 4.

*"A weird thing happened today,"* I began, and then recounted my story to Bammer, a friend from an online chat-room.

Bammer and I had been logging in to this space for a very long time, we'd never met in real life, just here, at the end of a blinking cursor.

I slurped at my coffee, still too hot, and disappointingly lacking in flavour due to the haste in which I had made it. I had been mid-conversation when I decided that caffeine was in order so I typed a line that I hoped would illicit some thoughtful replies, and lengthy responses. Message composed, I hit the enter key, long armed, as I stood up and lurched toward the kitchen…

…and had come back to find that immediately after my entry someone had spat out another far more interesting topic that was subject to long and heated responses, so either way I was off the hook. It did, however, make me regret not taking more time in preparation of my beverage, and I was just about to get up to rectify the problem in my coffee cup when Bammer invited me to a private chat room.

We did that a lot to get away from the general chat room environment, we rarely closed it out though, so often (as we were popular residents of this sometimes too-busy site) people would enter to see what we were doing, and we'd have to open another room to get away from it all.

I accepted the invitation and waited while the screen refreshed, leaving just me and Bammer in the side bar. I waited while some brief code popped up that explained that Bammer was password protecting the room.

We knew quite a lot about each other and were as close as any of the few people in real life that I've managed to call 'friend'. The last time we were in a private chat room together was when Bammer's mother died.

That time after the protection code was in place she had simply typed: *"Mary died".*

*"You going to be OK?"* I had typed back.

*"Yes... I just need some quiet, so I came, go and do other stuff if you want, but being closed out in this chat room just, I dunno, feels safe."*

I understood, and so we sat - Bammer, me, and a blinking cursor for 56 minutes.

Bammer: *"You still there?"*

Me: *"Yup. You ok?"*

*"Yes, thanks. Really, thanks."*

And then it was just my name in the side bar. We never discussed it again.

So it was with some nervousness that I sat, waiting for an explanation for the need of such privacy.

*"I don't know how to begin."*

*"From the beginning I guess,"* I replied.

*"I'm sending you a file."*

I waited while the file downloaded, then opened it and waited for the file to snap into crisp clarity –

and dropped my coffee as I recoiled from the machine.

Bammer had sent me an image file that looked to be scanned from an old text, but I'd seen those two circles before.

*"What the fuck, B?"*

*"Sorry, I was hoping to explain while the file went – but it was smaller than I thought sooo."*

*"Where did you get it?"*

*"I got it from someone, what's more important is that I think I know what it means."*

*"You know that was what they found on her body, don't you?"*

*"Yes, of course I do. I was following the trial via court transcripts... surprised they let that little chunk of information out,"* she said, then, *"We need to meet."*

In the five years we had been online together, this had never been suggested before. It just wasn't our thing. We hadn't told any untruths about ourselves, in fact Bammer probably knew more about me than anyone else, now that She was dead.

*"That's a pretty drastic step."* I said.

*"What I have to say is pretty drastic and anything that can be traced or tracked puts both you and me in jeopardy."*

*"Okay, when?"*

Glad that my satellite style of work meant I could go anywhere there was an internet connection, I was prepared to leave at once if I needed to.

*"It can't be any time this week, and you'll have to come to me as I can't travel anywhere too far from home."*

I realised that for all I knew about Bammer, I actually didn't know where she lived. I never had the need, we made comments as the seasons changed, and from what B said I always thought it sounded near to me.

*"How do you know how far I have to come?"*

*"Oh, I know where you live… that is part of the problem."*

# 5.

Turns out it was a seven hour drive the town where Bammer lived. Bammer had given me the address of a motel on the outskirts of town, and told me to email from my blackberry after I checked in.

*"Pay cash – do not use your credit card. Do. Not."* she had directed.

I sent the email and settled in to wait.

The motel was fine, probably built twenty five years prior, and remodelled at least twice since. It was clean though, the internet wasn't throttled, and there was complimentary beer in the refrigerator.

My phone blinked.

*"Turn out the lights at 9pm, I will be there soon after with pizza"*

*"Turn out lights?"* I fumbled into the phone's keyboard.

*"I'll explain. After. Please just do it."*

At 8.55pm I turned out the lights.

At 8.56pm my phone blinked. *"And the outside light please."*

I did, and 30 seconds later there was a knock at the door.

I opened it, and a shape bustled through – I could smell pizza.

"Close the door, hurry!"

I quickly shut the door and placed the chain across – and thought briefly how such a flimsy piece of metal was going to stop the hordes that I imagined had followed Bammer here.

I turned, and peered in to the gloom. Thankfully the room was not totally dark; the lights and billboard in the car park threw enough illumination through the thin curtains so that while Bammer was only a silhouette, at least I could see enough to get my bearings.

"Can I turn the internal lights on yet."

"That depends. I don't do this kind of thing, I prefer my own personal company, let's just eat pizza and talk, we'll worry about lights later."

"Bammer, this is weirding me out a little."

"This is nothing compared to how weirded-out you'll be when we are done, I won't hurt you, I just need it to be this way for now."

I sat on one of the two single beds, Bammer the other. I reached for the bedside lamp and Bammer's breath hissed.

"It's okay, I'm just moving the lamp so I can drag the table closer to put the pizza on it, if you don't calm down…."

"I told you, I don't see people often."

"Bammer, it's okay."

We ate pizza, and had a beer each, then I packed up the remaining slices for breakfast and got us another beer.

"B, this is all getting a bit creepy. I'm sure that you're aware I'd be a little jumpy given that I am in a motel room, with the lights off, speaking to someone whom I know but can't see, who summoned me here by showing me a symbol that I last saw as part of the evidence kit in the trial for the murder of my ex-girlfriend…."

"You need to breathe."

"Throw me a bone, would you?"

"I understand that this is out of the ordinary…."

"You've got that right."

"…I understand, but it just has to be this way for now. And really, how different is it to us chatting online and not being able to see each other, at least tonight we have been able to eat pizza in the same room."

"You can paint it any which way you like, but I'm still freaking out."

"I knew this would be a mistake, but we're here now and I really need you to trust me."

There was nothing else I could do. Sure, I was concerned by all the cloak and dagger bullshit, but I knew Bammer, and had up to that point trusted her. I wasn't sure why I was giving her such a hard time.

I'd given up on fear a few months ago. What I hadn't given up on was liking to be fully informed of whatever the hell it was that was going on at any given time.

"It's not about trust, Bammer, it's about a pretty unusual situation I find myself in."

"It's going to get even more unusual before we're done."

"I'm not sure I like or dislike the sound of that."

I got up and went to the bathroom. In my desire to wash my hands, I suspect that I left pizza sauce on everything I had touched as I felt my as I crossed the room. While peeing I heard the chain of the door being released, the turn of the handle and then the soft closing of the door. I came out of the bathroom to find the bedside lamp back in its place, and turned on.

My phone was blinking - an email from Bammer:

*"I'm not great with real life. I'm not frightened of you. Don't be frightened of me. I'll contact you tomorrow. Enjoy your breakfast pizza."*

I turned the light off again, and lay down on the bed to wait until sleep took me.

# 6.

At 9am there was a knock at the door. I had been sleeping heavily, so leapt at the comparative loudness in the gloom of my shitty-but-clean motel room.

I threw the door open, breathing in so that I had enough air to blast a verbal assault on the person who dared wake this bear from its slumber.

But there was no-one there.

A car was slowly cruising out of the parking lot, an everyday car, but with blacked out windows.

I looked outside the door and found an old archive style box, with its lid not quite flat on its cardboard rim and the cardboard handle inserts turned inward.

Rather than stand there staring at it, I bent and picked it up feeling weird that I was actively listening for ticking noises.

"What the fuck is going on with me?" I said as I stepped back into my room.

Inside was neatly sectioned in to free hanging files (the very things that made the lid fail to adequately do its duty) with a note, hand written, laying across the top: "This is just the beginning."

The files sent my heart racing. Initially they just looked like bank statements, albeit MY bank statements, well, mine and Hers. There were photos too, and transcripts of online communications, not just between Me and Her, but with Us and others.

There were analysed lists of things that had been delivered to our house, things that had been delivered to my previous house. Lists of phone numbers with annotations like "Pizza delivery" and "Valentines flowers".

It was all set out in a manner that had the information easily cross-referenced, but no real guide as to what the information was all about.

"Bammer obviously has something to do with this" I thought, so I set about hooking up my computer.

B had been correct about the internet; it was clean, fast, and came as part of the "executive room package", for which I was grateful. Most motels either have crappy, patchy internet, or they make you pay extra for it OR a horrid combination of the two.

I opened my email program, and then set about activating the server tunnel that disguised where my computer was logging in from. I wasn't the paranoid kind, generally, but had always been a little careful about who could tell where I was. I spat coffee over my screen the day someone sent me a link to a site that was a parody of one of the geo-location sites that awarded points to the user for checking in to new venues etc. The parody site was called "PleaseStealMyShit.com" and pointed out how vulnerable people are when their absolute location can be mapped on a minute by minute basis.

Using a VPN tunnel meant that I was safe from anyone knowing I was away from home, it also meant it took a little time to connect as I used a pretty elaborate VPN.

Thirty seconds passed, and the connection was almost secured. I found myself (not for the first time) pushing impatience aside by telling my inner Time-Nazi that a minute to log in is way less time than getting off my backside, driving to the post box, checking the mail and driving home.

At the end of that little internal diatribe the connection pinged in to full traffic mode and, there not being anything particularly pressing in my email, I hit the 'compose' button.

*B, a box has just been delivered do you know anything about it?*

*Me.*

Another knock at the door, softer this time, and a note was pushed under the door.

*I'll be back with more pizza at 9pm tonight.*

I opened the door but, weirdly, nobody was around.

Not having any idea where there might be a door I could stuff my own reply under, I sent an email.

*"Does this town have anything other than pizza?"*

No reply came, other than an acknowledgment that the email had been opened and read.

Without being asked, at 8.55pm I turned out the lights and sat on the edge of the still-made single bed, waiting.

I even went to the trouble of leaving the door cracked so Bammer could just walk on in.

At 9.05pm the door swung open, its rubber weather strip scraping the industrial looking carpet in the entryway, a shadow dashed through, and the door was firmly shut – chain rattling into place.

"You're late," I began in mock indignation.

"YOU are the one who didn't want pizza."

"You don't think that is a big ask given that I've eaten pizza for three meals running?"

"Hah! No I don't, you haven't been out today have you? I've brought supplies."

"Supplies for what?"

"I'll explain shortly, it will make a little more sense, maybe. For now though I brought noodles, I seem to remember you like seafood, so I got you prawn and mussels, if you're not happy with that you can have mine and I'll have yours."

"Or we could share"

"Do you think our relationship could stand it?" said Bammer, laughing.

"B, we're in a fucking motel, with the lights out…"

"Yes, yes, you covered all that last night." said B, and proceeded to hand out boxes of food and various accoutrements.

"It would be a lot easier if we could just turn on one light," I said.

"I'd really appreciate it if we could eat first, I'll turn on the light later, after we eat. You need to prepare yourself for how I look. I am hideous."

There was no humour in that last part, spat as it was into the space between us, I began in knee-jerk fashion: "It's not what's on the outsi…"

"Spare me. I know you are trying to be supportive, but when you see me, you'll understand. Let's eat."

We ate, and I negotiated that we should eat what we thought was half of our allocated dish, then swap, thus alleviating the who-would-prefer-what issue. At the appointed changeover time, I passed mine over, and received the other box in exchange – my new box had barely been touched.

Like the night before, I packed the takeaway food containers away – again having some left in reserve for breakfast, and sat back down and spoke in the direction of Bammer's shadow:

"I am going to the bathroom. Whatever is going on here needs the both of us to be in one room, as it seems you know something about this box that was delivered this morning. You still haven't explained to me the connection, *your* connection to the symbol you showed me the other night, the one that was found on Her body."

There was no response, so I continued:

"What I'm saying is that I would really appreciate it if you didn't bail on me like last night. I'd also really like it if you could get past whatever it is that you find so hideous, we are going to need some light to discuss what's in the box."

I didn't wait for an answer, and my tone wasn't bullying – just matter of fact – and I left for the bathroom.

As I closed the door, I heard movement. The front door opened, and gently closed. I turned the light on in the bathroom and finished washing up. I placed both hands on the sink and stared at the mirror in frustration, the face looking back was grimacing.

Whatever was going on was important, I had to find out who killed my girl, but the whole clandestine dark-and-shadowy thing was beginning to get to me.

I heard the front door open and close again.

The security chain was added. Someone was back in the room.

I turned the light off in the bathroom and was surprised to see light glowing from under the door, the texture of the linoleum flooring going from orange peel to nothing in the space of the light's weak glow.

I opened the door.

"Not yet," Bammer said.

I waited and heard furniture being moved.

"Okay, before you come out, I want you to know that I know you won't be able to help your reaction, so don't feel bad."

"I don't care Bam, you need to trust me, so let's get this done."

Rounding the corner I found Bam, sitting at the small desk in the corner. She was an attractive woman. Not a super model, not plain. Just an honest, lovely looking (if somewhat geeky) human being.

She was wearing blue jeans, converse trainers, and a long-sleeved jacket over a tight white t-shirt that had some witty comment about computer code on it. She also wore thick framed, hipster-geek issue glasses.

In short, she looked perfectly normal.

"So you're the stand-in until the hideous one shows up?" I asked.

"Don't make fun of me. This is the reason I don't DO face to face. The joking that follows to try to make me feel at ease DOESN'T make me comfortable. It fucking annoys me, just recognise that I am some kind of freak and get over it would you?"

I didn't know where this was going, but it had tipped the scales for me. On balance, my friend had a high level of crazy going on that I was prepared to overlook, but I just didn't know how to talk my way out of the confrontational space I found myself in.

"Bam, I don't know what's going on over there on your side of the desk, but you should know me well enough by now to realise I make a joke about everything. It was an off the cuff comment, I had no desire to piss you off."

She didn't say anything.

"I just don't find you repulsive," I said.

"I can't help the way I look, I just…" a tear ran out from under her glasses.

I moved around the desk to stand behind her, and gently placed my hands on her shoulders.

"Let's not start on such bad terms."

"Thanks," was all she said.

# 7.

I was glad she was facing away from me when she took her jacket off. I am sure that the initial shock of what was underneath would have been too hard to conceal, and her facing away from me gave me time to regain my composure. The scarring, a harsh network of slashes and marks, ran from her wrists to her shoulder. Some seemed fresh, their puckered scabs lining up next to the pink new skin of slightly older marks. Whether new or old, their neat and almost uniform positioning made me suspect that they were all self inflicted.

I didn't mention it, I figured I should wait, or simply avoid the subject altogether.

"Right," she said "Want to find out a pretty shitty thing?"

"Is it about Her?"

Bammer continued "Yes, it's about Her, but it impacts us all. It's about life after death."

"Oh. This is great," I began "All this cloak-and-dagger crap and now you're going to hit me up for some pop-culture-religious bullshit…"

"No, I'm not. And if you and I are going to get anywhere, you are going to have to learn to stop flying off the handle. Temper won't help," she said as she fingered a raised lump on the soft flesh of her inner arm.

"I'm sorry Bam. I'm just a bit twitchy is all."

"Bah, I'm sorry too – it is all a bit much for you at the moment, the secrecy and everything, I keep forgetting that for you this is new, I've got a long head start on you is all."

"A start on what?"

"She wasn't murdered by some random beach-goer. She was erased."

"What?"

"She was 'removed' if you will, by people who believe that erasing memory is one way of ensuring an efficient transition in the afterlife. If you decided to follow the same theory you would have to erase yourself and everything about your relationship in order for to meet her again in the transition."

"Bam, what the fuck are you talking about?"

"This is going to take a while, but you are just going to have to work with me."

*****

We sat either side of the desk for the next couple of hours, as Bammer showed me all the connections that were traceable, connections to me, and connections to Her.

Spending almost my entire life online has meant that I have been exposed to just about every conspiracy theorist scandal that had been virally disseminated. Most of the theories, at least from the early 2000's on, had something to do with a Huxley-Orwellian hybrid of Big Brother meets entertainment. No matter what angle the theory was coming from, the story didn't change: Big Brother wants you to be entertained, it wants you to consume news and opinions, and most of all it wants you to do as much of it via an online service as is possible.

Once the technology was made freely available (they said), Big Brother's desire was fed because Everyday-Joes were spending a great chunk of their lives online. So successful was this new world order (apparently) that figures came out stating that 99% of a regular person's time and life could be tracked. Like all figures, they seem not to be that far-fetched if you looked at them the right way. Even less so when they are supplied along with a compelling narrative.

Even knowing that I could be exposed to such scrutiny, I only ever treated discussions about conspiracies as an intellectual enterprise at best; discounting such theories as the ravings of paranoid geeks who had holed themselves up in their parents' basement.

My response was installing a VPN tunnel on my laptop, a piece of software that hides where my computer is logging onto the internet from. To eradicate attacks of a private nature from inside my computer I backed up the strength of anonymity the VPN offered by making sure I had the best virus detection software available, and that it was updated hourly.

I explained this to Bam.

"The VPN you use is fine, but it's only luck that you ended up with it. The virus software? Not great, even though it runs through the tunnel, it logs all your upgrade transactions, holds them and then the one time you forget, or can't be bothered waiting for your tunnel to load, it sends all of that information to its server. This information is then taken up by the companies interested in your movements and ID. There is enough evidence to suggest that the virus companies and their affiliates are spending millions every year writing virus code, releasing the code into the wild, and then after a few sacrificial servers have blown up with a heap of people's goodies on them, the companies come charging to the rescue with a solution. They get the info and they get masses of spill-over cash from people terrified that something awful might happen to them, this fear drives the consumer to purchase shiny new virus software or pay for an upgrade."

Bam paused and took a sip of her beer.

"But…"

"But why are people interested in you as a person? We're getting to that."

Another sip and she continued.

"Let's take this pizza order you made last year. November 6th."

"That was an anniversary. We, She and I, stayed in…"

"You order a lot of pizza, it could have been just another pizza night?"

"No B, I remember that date, because it was an anniversary. We always joked that should we ever be allowed to get married we'd do it on the 6th of November."

"Allowed?"

"It's complicated. It would be more than fair to say that her parents, particularly her father, weren't overjoyed with our union. There were other hoops we'd have to leap through too... same old things."

Not at all a description that did justice to our relationship, but as a snapshot it did pretty well. Her Father had done everything he could, both in private and in more public moments, to at first persuade and then threaten both of us in the hope that we would end it. It broke Her heart, but she consoled herself by waving her father's behaviour away as the ramblings of sick man trying to tie up any lose threads before the cancer finally took him.

To try to control the situation, She did her best to avoid any family gatherings so that he wouldn't have an audience for his ranting. Instead, she spent time with him on her own, calculating the cost of his demeaning rhetoric as a trade-off for her to be able to comfort him.

She always came back from these meetings ruined and partly broken. Even so, I never once tried to stop her going to him. Everyone had a role, mine was to rebuild and reinforce so that she was better prepared to weather the storm front she periodically walked directly into.

My explanation to Bammer was short, but I must have lingered in thought, the immense and familiar knot still tightly bound, the single thread that would undo it all eluding me.

Bam cleared her throat.

"Sorry," she said.

"Don't be, I'm almost numb to it now. Go on, you were saying?"

"Okay, I'll get on with it" she said, sipping her beer and placing it back on the moist beer ring on the desk.

"So this pizza you ordered, in fact *all* of the pizza you ordered, goes in to a data base and is listed by ingredient content. This information is then sold on to the ingredient wholesalers, who then determine the preferred toppings in your immediate area, so they can sell particular ingredients, like sausage for instance, to your local grocery store."

"Hardly earth shattering," I said, trying to get a grip on why Bam felt it important to tell me about the mechanics of pizza arrangement, all while fighting off the feeling that this was beginning to be a huge waste of time; time that might be better spent in a more productive enterprise, like work. I didn't care about the money I wasn't otherwise making, but I hated wasting time.

"That part isn't earth shattering, that's just good research," Bam continued. "If the information was used so that you would get a better deal at your grocer it'd hardly be worth mentioning. Although, recognising that we live in a capitalist society, and that the information collected and then combined with a solid dose of greed might actually pushed up the price in a specifically targeted is less than palatable. But this isn't necessarily about market forces and fresh products from a brochure filled with photos of happy smiling people eating a sausage. What it is about is when the companies have inferior product and they use this system to dump that product cheaply on to the market.

Remember all the salami scandals a few years back when a whole bunch of kids got poisoned by salmonella, or botulism, or whatever? 56 dead, and 200 ill. All of the product was traced to a meat plant that didn't even have a sales representative in the area. They did, however, have access to the sales stats from five different sources. They had product, they opened a new trading company, dumped the products and then shut the company. They had information and they dumped the product on a market that it knew would eat it, with liability aimed squarely at a company that didn't exist."

"Bam – this all sounds interesting, but really – isn't that just business?" I was fast losing interest.

The other thing about being professionally and recreationally online is while I found myself entertained by conspiracy folk, at least when I had had enough I could just turn the computer off. Bam was still here, and if she continued to crank into the beer, she'd be here for a while yet.

"You think it is business to murder 56 people and put a mass of other people in hospital?"

"No, Bam, but to find a place for your product to sell, THAT'S business."

"You don't see the danger in this, do you?"

"No, I don't, and I don't see how a pork product can be linked to Her being murdered."

"Okay," Bammer went on undeterred "Ever take photos with your phone?"

"Sure all the time, you've seen some of them, probably."

"You took photos of Her? Posted them online?"

"Occasionally."

"Your computer is walled off, but your phone isn't, every time you did that, you put faces to the phone number that ordered pizza. The face and phone number can be cross-referenced against any other credit card purchase made with the card. With the photo, they have a face. The number offers addresses…"

"P.O. Box."

"You think that the postal service isn't above serving up your real address? You know this stuff, or at least you've suspected it, or you wouldn't have taken such lengths to try to protect your privacy."

Bam emphasised this point with finger acted quotation marks on the word 'privacy'. "So… the companies cross-reference so that they, and therefore the government, knows everything about you, what you buy… "

This time for emphasis she grabbed up another folder of paper and scanned through its lines.

"….nice, I have one of these as well. 'bunny vibrator with rotating ball head – $69.95' …"

"That was a present for…"

"…and 'Wet stuff' personal lubricant 500ml – $19.95…'"

She was on a roll here –

"So with all that stuff they can profile you, your girlfriend, where you live, how you like to fuck, or get fucked, they can gauge how often you buy toilet paper and use that data for whether or not they need to add more commercials in your immediate area for high fibre diets. EVERYTHING IS CONTRIVED, nothing is in your control."

Bam drank the last of her beer and crushed the empty can, or at least squeezed it to deform its shape.

"Yes," I replied, doing my best not to show that, in my opinion, she was actually a nut job. "I haven't heard it explained to me in that much detail before."

"You don't have to take my word, once you have a chance to look through all this, it will become perfectly clear how in-depth it all is."

"Yeees, but Bam, what is the point of all this? How does this affect Her and why She was murdered?"

"The point of all this is that we are being remembered, too well, for too long. All of the data that remembers us, the data that we love so much because it makes life convenient? There are people out there that believe that such an intimate dossier of memories is trapping us here after we die. Essentially, they believe that all this," Bam waved her hands over the assorted documents between us, "means that people are unable to move on when they are supposed to."

"And what about Her? How does She fit in?"

"The people that killed her are obsessed with the theory that they are remembered when they die. By their loved ones, by co-workers… shit, they are concerned that they might be remembered by the guy at the coffee shop who gives them the same coffee every day. They believe that the natural process is supposed to be that a person dies, those that remember them die a few years later, and so when the last memory is gone from this earth they'll be able move on – those holding the memories are then bound in turn to the transient space while they wait for their loved ones and coffee shop guys to die and so on."

"Right… so, right now, if the theory is true, She is waiting for me to die or forget her."

"Yes. People have been postulating this tripe, or something like it, for centuries. Right now, those who have enough money are paying shed loads to have their lives erased. She was erased as part of that process."

I was sure that Bammer had a screw loose, but something in the way she spoke made me feel that this was more than just the musings of a crazy person. I resolved to at least look at the possibility of corruption with regard to the illegal use of the public's details. I was between writing projects anyway, having staved off a job to meet with Bammer.

Bammer stood up and said: "I need to use the bathroom, can you please go in and cover the mirror with something. I can't chance seeing myself."

"Bammer you…"

"Unless you want me to beer-piss in that pot plant right there, please, could you just go and cover the mirror."

"Okay, okay." I replied.

I went and opened the mirror cabinet, tucked a towel around it and tried to shut it again. The material got in the way of the hinge and made the mirror spring spongily back, but it seemed to hold the towel okay.

I left the bathroom and turned the corner and all but walked in to Bam as she had been standing in silence right outside.

We both said "Sorry" at the same time, and then stepped around each other; I made my way back to the desk with the file on it, she scurried into the bathroom.

"I'm turning the taps on so you don't have to hear me pee," she said

"What, you don't want me to hear you piss, but you were prepared to pee in the pot plant?" I called back.

"Can't hear you over the water," came the reply.

I was unsure of what my next move was to be. I had never been a religious person, or really given much thought to anything involving an afterlife. This had gotten all too weird.

Big-Brother-style corruption? Sure.

Big Brother-style corruption with the option to speed up your transition to an afterlife if you have enough cash? Fucking fruitcake-land.

The taps had been turned off, so I figured Bam would be out soon. I'd be polite, I still had a couple of questions, like where did all this stuff – the files in their neat little folders – where did it all come from? What was with the car driving slowly away when the box was delivered? Once I had something approximating an answer to my queries, I would sleep and then get the hell out.

\*\*\*\*\*

A shout came from the bathroom, followed by breaking glass.

I covered the four strides from the desk to the bathroom door and tried the handle – it was locked but thankfully felt flimsy enough so that if I had to channel my inner action-hero by forcing it, I could.

"Bam. Open the door."

Sobs leaked through the cracks in the doorframe.

"Bam, open the door please, whatever is going on in there you have to open the door. Or I'm going to have to force it open."

Still no answer, so I prepared to shoulder the thing open, I took two steps back and steadied myself...

The door handle turned, then released letting the door stand open an inch or so, the light from the low-watt bulb pushing a slash across the carpet, a shadow broke it then moved out of the way again.

"Bam?" I said, as I gently pushed the door fully open. "Shit."

She had sat back down on the floor, her hands bloody from a fresh gash on her arm. Bammer was holding a small shard of what was left of the mirror. Sobbing. Blood dropped in spatters on the floor in the triangle created by her crossed legs, a trail of blood-drops left a tidy dotted line mapping a path to and from the door, presumably from her opening it.

"Take it from me," she said, not looking away from the object in her hands.

The blood on the floor was pooling and beginning to seep in to the material of her jeans.

"What happened?"

"Take it away from me," she repeated through gritted teeth. She was passing the shard across the back of her forearm, a fresh stream of blood bubbled forth, dark and dripping from her elbow.

Grabbing at her hands meant that she stopped carving in to her arm, and I gently took hold of the piece of mirror, but Bam held it tightly.

"You have to let it go."

A look of significant inner struggle played across her face.

"Bammer" I said, with more force, but not unkindly, "Give it to me, let it go."

There was a pause, and then the resistance was gone and I nearly cut myself as my hand snapped away with the bloodied glass.

Bammer started to cry. Heaving, wracking sobs, as she gripped the fresh slash on her arm. The warm blood seeping slowly between her fingers, her tears splatting quietly in the pooled blood on the floor.

I crouched to comfort her and she leant into me, fully giving over to her sorrow, the move threw me off balance and I was flailing for something to hold on to, fearing I'd land on something sharp. I landed with my back propped up by the side of the bath tub, and we remained there, a broken mess, with me stroking her hair while I waited for the sobbing to stop.

# 8.

The carpark lights had just blinked out, and the world outside the motel room window was stuck in the time between dawn and day. Moments passed, but there was a stillness that remained, as if the day were summoning its strength before getting on with whatever it had in store.

Bammer was still asleep.

She hadn't had much to say after I had finally convinced her to stop crying. Apparently after she washed her hands she had gently tried to use the bottom of the towel covering the mirror to dry her them. As she pulled the towel gently toward her it had slid out from where I had haphazardly moored it. Her immediate response was to punch out at the mirror – so terrified she was of seeing her own reflection.

I had asked her about what happened next, with the shard and her forearm, and she had replied: "It's what I do. It will ultimately kill me, I fear. Some people have an idea of what will happen to them. I know I will bleed to death. All I can do to prolong this shitty life is to avoid seeing this." She pointed to her face as if pointing to a diseased animal that needed to be put down to end its suffering.

That's all she said. I helped her out to the desk and then retrieved her bag in response to her waving it toward her like it would come of its own accord. I placed the bag in front of her and she rummaged around with her free hand and pulled out a plastic lunch bag filled with gauze padding and bandages. She then placed her injured arm in front of me, and nodded toward it, indicating I should patch her up.

"This needs stiches. You need to go to a hospital."

She just shook her head indicating the negative, then laid it down on the bicep of her outstretched arm.

I did what I could, not ever having to actually deal with an injury before, I trawled the recesses of my brain to try to recall first aid information learned at a course years earlier.

Once done, she stood up, moved to the unused of the two beds, and removed her jeans.

Her legs made her arms look like untouched alabaster; so many individual scars on them that they looked like they been dipped in boiling oil up to the buttocks. She dropped her jeans to the floor, the heavy belt buckle making a muffled thump as it hit. Bammer did all this almost in slow motion as, in a daze, she crawled under the covers.

Seconds later, she was asleep.

I set about cleaning up the bathroom that at that moment looked like a murder had been committed. Careful to bag up as much of the glass as I could pick up without cutting myself, I then used the towel moistened with water to hand-mop the floor – hoping against hope that I had managed to find all the tiny bits of glass lying in wait to bury themselves into a soft and unsuspecting bare foot.

After the clean-up, and even though I didn't think sleep would come easily, I went to bed.

I knew Bammer as much as I could know anyone, I guess, but the night's events answered a lot of questions that had only manifested as a result of her actions in the bathroom; like the reason she hadn't ever uploaded any pictures of herself.

Bam had also never talked of having partners. She always commented on my relationship, but up until that moment I failed to see the great big gaping hole of information that was sitting, glaring at me from my memory banks.

I felt sorry for her, to be so miserable and unable to find a way out of it.

As suspected, sleep wasn't at all on the agenda, instead there was a protracted cycle of dozing and being jerked awake by brutal thoughts of blood and hammocks. On seeing the lights go out in the car park I got up and set about finding my running gear.

I needed to get out of the motel room to get some fresh air to help clear my head so that I could be at least a little more rational about what to do with Bam, the information she had brought to me, and the condition she was in.

I got undressed and pulled on my sports gear, then rose from putting on my shoes to find Bammer looking at me.

"Sorry," I said, a little uncomfortable about not knowing whether or not she had seen me naked. "I would have changed in the bathroom but, I figured you were asleep anyway…"

"If you've got something I haven't seen, then I think it's about time I saw it. Where are you going?

Literally running out on the crazy chick are you?" she said with surprising humour.

"Just a quick blat around the block, I like to start out my day with a bit of a sweat."

"Me too," she said, and I wasn't sure if that was sexually ambiguous statement or not as she pulled the cover up under her chin.

"Err… right. I'll be back in an hour. You'll be here?" I asked.

"Yes, I'll still be here, we have some other stuff to discuss, and then you should really start deciding what you are going to do next. Can't have you holed up here for all time now can we?"

I shook my head and reiterated that I would be back soon.

She propped herself up on her injured arm, and watched as I closed the door softly behind me, and left.

*****

I trashed myself during the run. From the time She was murdered until after the trial I ran until I puked, then ran home. Once, I passed out briefly in my own living room before I crawled to the kitchen and opened the refrigerator. I sat for the following three hours in the glow of the open fridge door, trying to eat and rehydrate, only getting up when I was sure that I wouldn't throw up any more.

This run, wasn't quite at that level of intensity, but I was breathing hard when I returned to the motel and realised that I hadn't taken the room key.

Standing on the worn doormat I was about to knock when the door opened a crack, then shut, followed by the noise of the chain being removed, then opened – a mirror of what happened last night with the bathroom door.

I tentatively touched the door, easing it open a little more. Bam's voice came through the gap, "I haven't wigged out again, I just don't go out in daylight unless I have a real need."

"If you are about to tell me that you think you are a vampire…"

Bam laughed, "No, I'm nuts, but I'm not THAT nuts." Bammer was behind the door and, once I was inside, she quickly closed it behind me and placed the chain back in its place.

"So you're here for the day then I guess."

"'Don't like to go out doesn't mean 'won't go out'," she said. "You trying to get rid of me? Can't understand why you'd want to. How many other people offer such unique entertainment?" she said, waving her bandaged arm around in the air.

"Entertainment I'd rather not have front row tickets for again," I replied.

"I'm sorry about that, it's beyond my control I'm afraid. Time to move on though…"

"Please don't do that again."

"I can't promise that, all I can do is try to put mechanisms in place that don't expose me. That I can promise to do, you don't think I enjoyed last night do you?"

"No."

"Let's move on then."

# 9.

In the time I had been away, food and fresh coffee had somehow materialised in the motel room.

Except for one folder, all the other files had been put away.

The folder sat on the desk between Bam and me as Bam poured me coffee and lifted a plate cover from the room service trolley revealing eggs, bacon and toast. All of which were my favourites. Indeed the bacon and bread were my preferred brand.

"I get it. All this technology and invasion of privacy is so you can get the bacon I like. Am I right?"

"It's not all evil now then, is it?" Bam said.

"What's this?" I asked, pointing with my fork at the file. It had Her name on it.

"That is where things get a little creepy. It's all the photos from the case."

"I don't want to see them," I said, pushing myself away from the desk

"It's not as bad as you think. The twin sign, the sign I showed you that got you all interested in coming here, actually serves an interesting purpose."

"What? Apart from freaking me out?"

In patient tones Bammer explained that the sign is a placeholder or call out sign designed to be traced by elaborate software, and connected to the massive matrix of data sets already criss-crossing the lives of everyone. Its sole purpose had little to do with the murderer, and everything to do with the murdered.

Once the software found evidence of the sign, it would hunt, back-link and list everything and everyone to do with that single file. Once the list was produced a secondary mechanism systematically found and destroyed the files. If the files were too obvious to be removed, they were altered in a way that would allow them to remain in the public eye, but within a short space of time a virus would change the file, little by little, every day, until it was unrecognisable in comparison to the original.

The mechanism had obviously started to work, as the photo I was looking at Her name on it or at least a misspelled version of Her name. The photo could have been anyone, but it certainly wasn't Her anymore, as the image had changed along with the name.

"That file was printed out two days ago, it will be different again now. The change stops after about six months."

"This still doesn't explain why she was murdered."

"It kind of does. The files can be easily altered or deleted, and photos like that aren't the kind of thing that are put in a frame and hung over the mantelpiece. Generally, any images that are printed only last so long and are often destroyed simply to make space in filing cabinets and desk drawers. Sadly, it is the way of the world that rather than go and find the old prints, people tend in this situation to print out new ones. Because it's easier. The new photos become the new reality, and before long the essence of the subject is gone."

"But, murder?"

"The problem is that people don't change. Files, yes, but flesh and bone people don't. There are viruses aimed at infecting people's lives to make them want to change, but they are hard to control because these little nasties simply change the way a person feels about themselves and, as a result, the way they look. But that only affects the individual. Without the benefit of being able to reset the mind, a person can't be quietly changed. They need to be erased in order to close out their memories." Bam was fingering the scars on her arm as she spoke, eyes slightly glazed.

She blinked a couple of times and then continued, "Someone was contracted to erase your girl. Someone she knew, or thought she knew, paid a lot of money to have her and others killed."

"If it is true that she was killed for some quasi-religious purpose, why bother with the file? She wasn't the one who feared being stuck on earth."

"Respect, and some remorse. Apparently it is quite common. To help alleviate the guilt of murdering an innocent, an extra fee is provided to begin the erasing process for the one murdered, so that they don't have to wait in the afterlife. If they have enough money they might also include the immediate family of the victim. That would be you."

My head spun.

"If all that is true, how did you get hold of the files?"

"We got hold of the files before too much could be altered. We left a trap when our software pulled up the symbol in Her records, and watched as they set about unleashing their various viruses into the file. Anything that the virus took an interest in, we did too."

All of a sudden the windows in the front of the old room looked too big, and the door too flimsy.

"We? Who the fuck is 'WE'?"

"WE are a few individuals who used to be part of that machine. We're scattered around the globe. Although it would be fairer to say that I am almost the entire drive behind this new group – the rest of 'us' I utilise as researchers. They are, for all intents and purposes, drones for hire. Though, what we share is a common interest in deep data; it's how we knew where and how to look. We were hunter-programmers, virus gods, and some of the things we found ended up badly for those tied to the things we found. In short, we were workers within The Movement."

I looked at her again and wondered how the hell I had allowed myself to get dragged into this.

"This motel is the safest data zone in the world. You don't have to stay here forever, but it's a good place to start from. The phones are routed through tunnels that are hyper-encrypted – the military has nothing on us. Same with the Internet – there is a cash machine that is restocked but all transactions are untraceable. You can go, but the questions that you are no doubt thinking to ask people will throw up so many flags you'll be dead before the week is out. Or by the end of the month if you have your wits about you."

I got up, grabbed my laptop, and started to stuff everything I brought with me into a bag.

Bammer did nothing but tap a few keys on her phone, then set it down.

"We are...I am on your side, you don't need to fly into a panic. While you are here, you are safe – if you leave this place we don't have the man-power to cover you."

"So I'm a fucking prisoner now?" I replied as I grabbed my sports stuff and jammed it into another bag. "In a motel in outer-west butt-fuck? That's just great."

"You need to calm down, it's not ME who wants you dead. I like you. Particularly now that you've seen me at my worst, I thought we had a connection..." she came over and ran a finger up my arm. "I..."

"I'm not your type." I opened the door and walked out to my car. Someone had left a note on it.

*"What your morning run looked like before I changed it... No. Don't thank me."*

Below the typed sentence was a mapped image of the exact route I took during my run this morning. Bam must have guessed at what would happen after this morning's discussion, and had left this little piece of electronic stalking on my car while I had been in the bathroom.

I turned back to look at the door of the motel room, a short distance away. Bam was standing one pace out into the daylight. "You run using a GPS enabled watch. You bought it with a credit card. With only a few keystrokes that information can be found. I changed it, not so much to protect you, but to protect this site."

I didn't know what to do. I felt I was in danger, I just didn't know from whom.

I got into the car and just sat, gripping the steering wheel. Bam walked into the motel reception keeping to the shadows. She caught the still closing door as she exited again, walking toward me with something in her hand.

When she had got to within a body length of the driver's door, she turned, and backed toward the car. I realised she was avoiding any chance of seeing her reflection in the window or paintwork. She stepped slowly backwards until she made contact with the car, and using her free hand slapped gently in the window.

"You really need to take what I've got here, it's mostly yours anyway."

I wound the window down, and she passed the package to her free hand and then backwards, still without looking, adding a slight frustrated shake to let me know I should take it.

"Are you trying to be a cliché?" I asked, "A package, with what I guess is money in it, am I on some B-grade hidden camera show?"

"No," said Bammer, "the cash isn't a donation, I ghosted it out of your account."

"Ghosted?"

"It's your money. The amount I withdrew still looks like it is there, but we've locked the amount out, like a cheque waiting to be cashed. Take it or don't, but it's your cash anyway. The cliché is that with the cash is a gun. A lovely black 9mm pistol, you might need it."

With that, Bam dropped the package in my lap. I jolted at the thought of a loaded gun in free fall in front of my vulnerable and easily blown-a-hole-in body.

Bammer was already walking away when I had recovered, and I watched her retreat into the office. I was alone in the parking lot, not entirely convinced about leaving or staying. As a stalling tactic, I decided to check the parcel. As promised, there was a gun in there, lying on the top of the neatly bundled cash, like something from the cover of a crime novel.

I have no fear of guns, I quite like them actually – not because I have ever had the desire to shoot anyone, I just like the precision of the machine, not its potential. In fact, I could happily fondle the firing mechanism of a gun and be completely enthralled by it.

I was strangely concerned by the cash, even if it was allegedly mine. At a guess, there was probably about five grand in total. Carting around that amount of currency would make anyone twitchy.

"Maybe I will need a gun," I said to myself, and then immediately chastised myself for so easily adopting the idea of gun ownership so wholeheartedly.

Stowing the cash and gun in my satchel, I got out of the car, and retraced Bam's footsteps across the cheap asphalt lot to the motel office.

A clinical-sounding electronic bell went off as the door opened and the old man who had checked me in the other night was behind the counter, looking like he hadn't moved.

"Can I help you?"

"I need to speak to… Bammer?" I said, feeling foolish at not knowing Bammer's real-life name; a feeling compounded by the lingering thought that old people find online names foolish anyway.

"I don't know any 'Bammer'," he said, emphasising the name.

"Okay. Then the girl who came in through that door before, about three minutes ago."

"No girl came through here."

"Yes, yes she did," I stammered

"Don't tell me what did or didn't happen youngen', I've been behind this counter for fifty years, I'd know whether someone came in that door or not."

"Okay," I said, "How bout I settle up for my room then," hoping that might give me more time to coax Bam out of the shadows.

"You haven't checked in yet, no-one's checked in for about a week," he said looking at me like I was the crazy one in this conversation. "You can't check out if you haven't checked in."

My phone vibrated in my pocket, a message had come through.

"*Just go, he doesn't have a usable memory. He's my Dad, he has a disease that has caused him to have no short term memory. He thinks it's 1965, all the time. If you are going to go, then just go, don't use any other phone than this one. It's cleaned and tunnelled now, along with your laptop, did that while you were running. I'll call you when you get into your car.*"

I apologised to the old man for disturbing him, and left, the door ding donging as it opened.

The phone was ringing before I made it to the car. I answered but the light breeze was making it too hard to hear.

"Just let me get in the car, I can't hear what you are saying." The call disconnected. The phone went off again as I shut myself inside my sun-warmed car.

"Hello, I don't have a lot to say," I said.

"Where will you go?" Bam's voice.

"I'm going to the beach, I want to speak to some people…"

"Going to rat us out are you? Feel like broadcasting the location of a weird little motel where you were lured to…"

"No, surprisingly, I'm not, I want to speak to the police that arrived the day She was killed."

"I guess this is one way of you seeing that this isn't some fantasy land I've been talking about."

"What do you mean?"

"You'll have to find that out for yourself. I have taken the liberty of changing your license plates to erased ones, so the traffic cameras won't be able to trace you. Of course they'll still waypoint the car but they won't be able to tie it to you. Wear a hat, and sunglasses at all times. The road cameras have been capable of High Definition imagery for years, don't get me started on CCTV."

"Thanks, I guess."

"I'll be here when you need me, be careful."

I pulled out into traffic and at the first intersection the lights were red. All of a sudden I was acutely aware of all the visual recorders just at one intersection. I quickly pulled on my sunglasses and a baseball hat that had been in residence under the passenger seat since I bought the car. Crumbs and beach sand cascaded out of it as I pulled it low over my brow, the action making me feel only a little less exposed.

# 10.

It took five hours to get to the beach. The feeling was unsettling as I pulled into the drive and coasted around the back of the little cottage.

It was closing on four o'clock in the afternoon, and the grassed area at the back of the house looked as well kept as ever. The local football club had a scheme that allowed holiday house owners to pay a yearly fee, giving work to the young players along with some much-needed funds that all rural sports teams need to find.

The guys who looked after this place could take on a career in horticulture if the whole football thing didn't bear fruit.

I noticed that one of them had kindly replaced the string hammock with a fabric one, and I felt like it was an apology of sorts from the town. A token against what had happened in their quiet little spot on the coast.

Apology or not, on balance I was grateful that it had been replaced; having the empty frame sitting square in the middle of the yard would have served as a greater reminder of the horrible thing that had happened there. Not that I would consider using it of course, but the gesture was welcome.

I moved from the car to the back step, and remembered the last time I had looked over the back yard. When She was alive, and beautiful, and mine.

"And she was right there," I said. A fat tear escaped and ran down my face, hung briefly on the point of my chin, then detached and fell to the step. 'Phat', the old timber drank it greedily.

*****

There had been a large supermarket on the highway about an hour from the motel and given that all the talk of monitoring had made me twitchy about who I might run into, I had taken the opportunity to stock up on supplies where I was unlikely to be recognised.

I didn't need much, as it was my intention to only stay a couple of days to see if there was any sense to be made about what the hell was going on.

Putting the shopping bag down on the bench, I set about unloading its contents. Optimistically, they included the makings of salad sandwiches, should I decide for something approximating a healthy snack. More realistic were the other contents of the bag – cans of baked beans and spaghetti – primarily to cover the likely event I didn't want a salad sandwich. At least there was something I could eat that didn't involve me calling town for pizza.

Lastly, I pulled two large bottles of tonic out of the bag. If there was ice still in the freezer it would be a sign that I should have the gin and tonic I had made, but didn't drink, all those months ago.

Grimacing in case of bad-ice-situation news, I threw open the freezer door and, miraculously, there was ice in the tray. Although the tray was only half full, there was enough ice for a tall glass, I'd just have to pray to the freezer gods that they could get the next batch frozen in good time.

The ice, while adequate, filled less of the glass than I had intended, so I took that as a sign to add more gin and resolved the conflict by telling myself I was drinking for two. Figuratively.

*****

The ice clacked in the plastic high ball. She had purchased a set of six of these tumblers at the store in town, citing that Perspex, while not romantic, was practical. She then went on about my history of dropping more delicate glassware in friend's backyards, and she had a point.

I smiled while remembering her unerring sense of practicality, and leaned against the counter as I sipped at my drink. My smile diminished as the kitchen seemed to shimmer, a humid haze washing across my vision brought her back again to the kitchen she adored.

The new version of Her unpacked the glasses, while blood streamed in gouts from the back of her head. "I'm going out back, I'll be waiting on the hammock, don't be long?" she said, her voice restricted by the gurgling blood leaking from the bottom of her jaw. She covered her mouth and coughed; more dark ooze filled her hand and leaked through her fingers.

She just wiped her hand on her shirt, itself a sponge for what was seeping from the hole in her upper chest. Grinning at me in what was once such a beautiful smile, now some macabre grimace – the borders of her teeth blackened, and putrid.

*****

I woke up on the couch in the small lounge room at the front of the house, the gin bottle open and empty, lying on its side. I remember giving up going to and from the refrigerator for the tonic - the seven or so steps to the kitchen becoming some kind of imposition - so I had simply brought the gin and tonic bottles to the coffee table. Part of the annoyance came, I think, from the disappointment of half-frozen ice.

The refrigerator had obviously turned against me, so in some kind of human vs. appliance protest I figured my tonic was too good to be in it.

The only benefit that came from this was that in my startled wakefulness I had a half bottle of tonic within arm's reach to rinse out whatever baked and scaly horror was in my mouth. It took three large gulps before I realised that sometime before passing out I must have decided that I could cut out the inconvenience of pouring my drink into a glass by simply pouring the remaining gin directly into one of the tonic bottles, thus killing two birds with one stone.

A plan that must have seemed perfectly reasonable at the time but, like a juniper and quinine booby trap, had come back to bite me.

The final gulp sprayed across the coffee table. I fumbled to put the lid back on and got up with the view of finding something non-alcoholic to drink, then immediately thought better of it. I lay back down on the couch, my head pounding, the windows still dark.

*****

I woke with a start. Light was just beginning to peek through the meshed curtains; orange abominations that must have been in place for as long as the house had stood. Curtains that were so awful that we had decided to leave them hanging in a homage to 70s decor.

I'd been dreaming about Her again. Not as she used to be, rather how she would look now. Rotting and oozing.

The dream didn't wake me though. In my sleepy haze, I was sure a noise had brought me from my slumber.

Gingerly, I went to the kitchen and marvelled at how, despite my being in the house for less than a day, the place already looked like a municipal dump. I entered the kitchen tentatively, just in case the apparition from the evening before had decided to reprise its performance, and was weirdly surprised that there was no blood on the bench; no ruddy brown footprints exiting the kitchen.

There must have been a noise. I slept heavily at the best of times, and like a rock when drunk. The back door was creaking, swinging gently open, a cool breeze passing through and refreshing me slightly as it crawled across my gin-sweat face. I moved to the door and opened it fully, the wire screen door was still closed, and after the usual procedure it opened, freeing me from the house's stale interior.

There was someone in the hammock, or there appeared to be. I rubbed my eyes and took a couple more steps toward it. The breeze caught the fabric of the hammock and it swayed gently, as if someone had just readjusted their position. I moved closer, and heard my name on the breeze; whispered, quiet. I could smell Her, the sweet smell she had, mixed with a summer perfume. Then a gust came and the hammock filled violently like a yacht's spinnaker.

The hammock frame unmoored itself, violently pulling the anchoring pegs out of the ground. The sail deflated as the frame tumbled over and the mirage was gone, but left the hint of something familiar, something I couldn't put my finger on. I was weeping as I righted the hammock, and sat in it, trying to coax any life that she had left behind to make itself known, begging the empty space to comfort me.

The whispering on the breeze had changed to a soft and gurgling giggle. I stood on the place where She had died. The grass showing no sign of the life that leaked into it.

# 11.

My phone was blinking when I returned to the quiet of the house. Putting it to the side, I set about cleaning up the sticky residue of the mistaken tonic incident, then turned my attention to the kitchen, taking too much time to clean the bench where her apparition had stood, very much aware that I was trying to clean something that wasn't there. There was a settling nature in putting the house back to order, the cleaning gave me a renewed focus on what it was I had returned for.

Engrossed as I was in the almost ritualistic action of wiping and scrubbing, it took some time before I paid attention to my phone again. Blinking quietly, it was indicating that a text message was waiting.

It was short: *Please check email – Bam.*

I tethered my phone to my laptop and went to my email program. Whatever Bammer had done to my equipment it had certainly improved it – I'd never seen download speeds so fast.

*You're probably amazed at the speed of the Internet now aren't you? The tunnel takes off all the limiters put in place by servers and internet company administrators to throttle information. It's a form of control, and works on the theory that slower information is easier to edit on the fly.*

*I guess you haven't been out to see the police yet. I really hope you find what you are looking for. Just be aware that things are changing every minute, Her file has changed so much that, as an individual, She is unrecognisable as the person you once knew.*

*Call me when you get a chance, I want to talk about what happened at HQ when you were here. I can't help what happened with the mirror and I can't really help how I feel about you. I know it's weird, I know you're probably freaked out, and I never expected to get attached in a physical way with you. But I did. On second thoughts, don't call me, I don't have much more to say than that.*

*If you need my help, please just let me know. But one more time for the record – do not connect with anyone if not through either your personal phone or your laptop. It's just not safe. People are looking for you. Judging by the quality of the changeling-virus they let loose in Her file, they are some pretty heavy hitters.*

*B xx*

I understood that Bammer thought I was in need of help and protection, but surely if the people involved in Her death were after me, they'd already have taken me out by now.

This always seemed to be the biggest flaw in conspiracy theorists ideas. If they were such a heavy link in the information chain why weren't they either: 1. Recruited by the 'enemy' to use their talents for subversive motives or 2. If the information they were privy too was so damaging, really, why weren't they already dead?

I couldn't verify anything that Bammer had said was true. I didn't have access to the highly protected files she could allegedly view at a moment's notice. I could only take Bam's word for it and, given that Bammer wasn't the most stable person on the planet, surrounded as she was by her self imposed data vortex, I didn't know what weight her word carried.

I went to the bathroom, and walked into a memory of Her. All Her toiletries were still here – her toothbrush and after-shower moisturiser still in their place on the terribly out-of-date vanity. I got in the shower with a view to having not much more that a rinse, but the memory of Her was even stronger here.

\*\*\*\*\*

The morning of Her murder she had demanded I join her in the shower, insisting I wash every part of her. Then she gently reciprocated, her hands and mouth making me gasp and grip at the rail as my knees tried to buckle underneath.

"Fuck me. Fuck. ME! I want to come. I want to come now," she said as she positioned herself, already working hard on getting a head start on what she was asking me to do.

Just like then, the water was beginning to cool, my desire for a fast shower overcome by memory.

"Fuck me," a hissing whisper.

I felt hands on my buttocks and, startled, I slipped falling hard against the wall of the shower. The shower curtain billowed in and then formed the shape of Her, naked, reaching for me.

The curtain collapsed, and I shivered at both the memory, and cold water spraying over me.

# 12.

The police station was a typical rural outpost. The most action it saw was on the odd Friday night when one of the local bars got a little rowdy and some of the regulars had to be shipped to the drunk-tank to sleep it off.

The station was probably of similar vintage to Bammer's motel. The timber weatherboard matched just about every other building in the town, but what separated it as something more than just another small-town structure was its concrete path to the door, and security grating on all the windows. The cells were at the back, and made of the clean brickwork that government buildings seem often to employ. They were a relatively new addition to the station; deemed necessary after someone, also drunk, tried to help their brother escape by setting fire to the outer wall of the old timber cell block.

Other than that, it was quite an accommodating building as police stations go, and I waited in the front-desk area, while an old woman pleaded her case about her neighbour.

"But she is stealing my apples!"

"Mrs Grey, the apples you are talking about are on a branch overhanging her side of the fence. They are actually her apples."

"But it's MY tree, my husband's ashes are under that tree, so my husband is IN those apples. That woman tried to get at him while he was alive, there is no way I'm allowing her to put him in her mouth now he's dead."

The police officer looked over at me, while I turned away to hide my smirk.

"What are you laughing at, John?" the old woman said, addressing the police officer, who was barely keeping his mirth in check.

"Nothing, Mrs Grey, I'm just a naturally happy looking fellow, I guess. Tell you what, how about I come over and prune that old tree for you, then your husband won't be hanging his apples over your neighbour's fence."

I stifled a laugh and pretended to look at my phone when the old woman briefly looked over at me.

"I won't be paying you, you know, this is a legal matter, and you are the law," said Mrs Grey.

"I know that, but perhaps you could see your way clear to making me a cup of tea after I'm finished?" said John.

"Well, I guess so. When can I expect you?" she said.

"I'll be there tomorrow afternoon around four o'clock. Does that suit?"

"No later than that, I like to have my dinner at five pm," said a placated Mrs Grey.

"No problem, I'll be there before four tomorrow." he replied.

The old woman turned and, with a look of victory, strode out the door, turning just before she left to say, "You had better like apple pie too, I'm not going to spend my afternoon baking you a pie if you aren't going to eat it."

With a final flounce she was gone.

"Hi," I said as Officer John indicated it was my turn, a redundancy at best as I was the only other person in the waiting room. I approached the counter and he offered his hand and shook mine, warmly.

"What can I do for you?" he asked.

"I was hoping that I could ask some questions about a murder here a few months ago?" I asked, my voice catching in my throat.

"There was a murder here?"

"Yes, that's right," I said, and gave Her name and the address of the beach house.

He went through a door saying that he would check the files. He looked excited that something so dramatic had happened in his sleepy town.

In a short time he returned, looking at a file as he approached the counter, "I've only been here a month or so, so I'm sorry if I'm sounding a little vague. I've checked the main server, and there was a murder here a few months ago, but not anyone with that name. It also appears that the case was resolved. I don't have the hard files, they haven't come back from town."

I was surprised and a little concerned, but after the events of the last few days I wasn't entirely unprepared.

"Perhaps I could speak to the officers who worked that case? Officers Michaels and Dane?" I suggested. Whoever was behind the defiling of Her records might be able to change the files, but they couldn't yet change people's memories, could they?

John's face sagged slightly.

"You won't be able to speak to them, this is a rotating post, as the department thinks it's better if the police officers don't go too local. They worry it might soften their approach to law enforcement. They got posted out when I got posted in, and I'm still waiting for my second officer to be named."

"Where have they been posted to? Perhaps I could go to them," I said feeling the need to leave – too many coincidences. My thoughts on Bammer's apparent paranoia diminishing and giving way to plausibility.

John said, "Well I guess you couldn't know." He took a breath, "Dane and Michaels shipped back to their home towns and, within a day of each other, Dane was killed in a car accident, and Michaels took his life as a result. They became like brothers during their time here. A real shame."

I took a step away from the counter. "Well it seems I have hit a dead end then, I'll just get out of your way, you've got a lot to do I guess, working on your own and all."

"You've got that right, perhaps I can get your number and my supervisor can give you a call?" said John, taking up a pen and paper.

"I'm... I'm just in the process of changing phone companies, so my number won't be any good and reception at the house is lousy. I don't want to be a bother. Thanks, Officer John," I replied and took another step away from the counter, "Really it's no problem, hope your apple pie is good tomorrow".

I turned and left, moving quickly along the still morning-damp path to my car. I got in and pulled into the quiet street. John appeared in my rear-view mirror, standing on the front porch of the station and shading his eyes against the morning sun as I drove away.

It was too much to wave the morning's findings away as mere coincidence, and Bammer's theory started to appear to have some merit after all. What was clear is that I was exposed, and had real desire to get away from the beach.

# 13.

For the second time in as many days, I drove down the side of the house and parked. The hammock was still in place, my re-pegging had anchored it properly, although there hadn't been any real wind to test it.

Even so, I walked close to the hammock to check my handiwork, noting the proximity of the new pegs to the old holes, the earth, brown and wormy in the ruts that were torn up when it had uprooted itself the previous night.

There was a dark stain in the centre of the sling, dark against the lighter fabric. It hadn't been raining, yet the hammock had enough water in it to make it sag, the stain obviously the most saturated area and where the water was seeping through.

I shuddered, feeling cold all of a sudden, and unhooked one end of the fabric, then the other, emptying the water. The screen door slammed just as the small shackle swung and clanged into the hammock frame, startling me. With a gasp I turned to the swinging door, its dusty bug-mesh distending as if a hand were pushing against it – I blinked, rubbed my eyes, and it was gone.

I ran up the stairs and into the house. Someone had been there. My travel backpack was empty and torn at the seams. The old coffee table we had purchased from a thrift store last year was upended and laying on its top, displaying its truly ugly legs as they pointed upward like a Jacobean cockroach.

Even though I had taken it with me to the police station, I reflexively felt the satchel at my side, and rummaged around in it to make sure everything was still there. Panic had set in, and so had unreasonable thought: Could whoever had done this to the living room have snuck up on me somewhere in the last couple of hours, stealing the only things that could keep me safely connected?

The phone and laptop were still there, but my hand moved to the zippered inside pocket, then reached in, my hand curling around the cold grip of the gun.

A hand fell upon my shoulder, and I spun around thoughtlessly pointing the gun at the newcomer; my hands shaking so much that if I had let off a round it would have been a miracle if it had gone anywhere near my intended target.

"Woah there," a newly familiar voice said. It was John, and he was backing toward the kitchen door, one hand in the air and one hand on his police belt, as if preparing to unclip something.

I immediately lowered the gun. "It's not loaded," I said, showing him the empty chute where the magazine should go.

"Fine, just stop waiving that thing around will you," he said, as he relaxed both his hands.

"The door was wide open when I arrived and I was going to call out, but noticed that the kitchen was a mess, wait, it IS a mess isn't it? It's not just how you live, is it?" he said.

I drew my free hand across my forehead. "No, I'm not a clean freak, but that is definitely not my doing," I said, placing the gun back in the satchel pocket.

"What happened?" John asked, "Did you surprise anyone when you arrived?"

"The door slammed when I arrived, but I think that might have been the wind, or a ghost," I replied.

I didn't think John was taking much notice of what I said, and hoped the ghost reference would just slide by. It hadn't though.

"Don't think that there would be any burial grounds this close to the water, so I think we can rule the ghost hypothesis out," said John with a wry smile.

I felt more at ease, and John set about looking for anyone that might still be in the house, his hand back to resting easily on his belt. I let him go about his business, but in reality, I didn't think he would find anyone.

I went to the kitchen and cleared a space to place two coffee mugs down on the bench.

"I'm going to make coffee," I called out.

"Is now the time to make coffee?" John called in reply.

"You just keep on doing what you do best, I'll do one of the things that I do best: make awful instant coffee" I said loud enough to be heard, but without shouting. She used to remind me of that all the time.

*****

"No matter where in this house I am," she would say, "I'm never more than a couple of dozen footsteps away, so STOP SHOUTING." The last would be said with her nose against mine. Then she'd kiss me. It turned into a pantomime, she knew I was shouting on purpose, she knew it was going to end in a kiss, or like on the morning of her death, more than a kiss. Right there, the last time I tasted her was right there on the island bench in the kitchen.

We bought the place almost entirely based on the kitchen. It was huge and the large bench in the middle served as a breakfast bar, cocktail bar and book stand. The real-estate agent had walked outside to make a call when She kicked her shoes off and got up on the island bar, legs akimbo, skirt riding up to display the underwear I always loved to see her in.

"…and, it seems to be the right height. We might never make it out of the kitchen," She said "where's that realtor gone, I want to find out if he'd just sell us this bench, and then throw the house in for free."

*****

"No," the voice startled me. It was John.

"No, what?" I said, shocked to be back in the room, and again reminded that She was not, nor ever would be here again.

"No one here," he said as I handed him a cup of black liquid.

"Milk is in the fridge, sugar is in that bowl there," I indicated the awful pelican shaped sugar bowl we had picked up at a car boot sale last summer.

"So what do you think happened?" asked John, stirring vigorously at his coffee.

"I don't know, obviously someone was a little critical of the way I had my house arranged," was the best I could come up with. I wasn't comfortable exploring the potential that whoever had murdered Her could theoretically be coming after me now.

The concept that I had come to think of as 'Erasure' was well beyond my ability to speak of.

"Might it have something to do with why your car registration, while valid, doesn't actually go anywhere." he said, probably coming to the reason he found himself here in the first place.

Stalling, I replied, "What do you mean, 'it doesn't go anywhere'?"

"I mean I ran your license plate after you left just as a matter of procedure and the car doesn't actually have an owner or registered address. It's either the biggest glitch in the history of the registration system, or you're some kind of secret agent with friends in high places," he said, in a tone that wasn't accusing, but more bewildered than anything else.

"Must be a glitch then," I said.

"Some glitch."

"Yes. Indeed. So is that what brought you here then?" I asked, trying to move the conversation to safer a safer subject.

"No. I figured that since you came in looking for a murder file that doesn't exist anymore I would come out here and check for myself. You don't look untrustworthy. I just thought I'd better be certain that it wasn't some weird new way of working out information about holiday residences or something. I half expected to come out here and find the place full of surf-squatters, or high school kids smoking pot, or something."

"No, Officer…"

"John is fine."

"No, John. Nothing as interesting as that."

"You aren't really setting my mind at ease. This is a holiday town. The people who live here year round like that you holidayers bring cash into the town's businesses, but they don't like this kind of stuff" he said indicating the damage to the beach house.

"I didn't ask for this to happen, John, just like I didn't ask for Her to be murdered. This is NOT the idea I had when we bought this place." I changed my voice to that of a new house buyer: "Oooh sweetheart, this is the perfect place, and now that we've bought it, you just sit there quietly while I go inside to make us a drink, it'll make it easier for whoever is watching us to sneak over here and put a fucking bullet through your head…"

I realised that I was losing it. I thought I was okay. But something had switched and I was now obviously angry.

"You need to calm down," said John.

"I need to get the fuck out of here, is what I need."

"That might be so, but I'd appreciate it if you could stay until tomorrow morning, I really need to sort out what the hell is going on with your license plate."

"I'm not staying, you can have my … number and email, but the best thing I can do is get out of town. Better for you, and by the looks of what happened here when I was gone, much better for me too I suspect."

I managed to avoid saying 'my safe number', John already looked on the verge of suggesting we go down to the station to talk about things.

He didn't, though.

"Where are you going then?" he asked.

"With respect, John, I'd rather not say. Unless you have some legal reasoning for knowing my whereabouts?" I said.

"No, that's not why I was asking. I just wanted to make sure you have somewhere to go. You appear a bit agitated. Too agitated actually to be driving any great distance."

I sat down on one of the stools and put my head in my hands.

"I know, I know. It's probably three parts what has happened here today and one part hangover. I'll be okay."

"Don't leave," he said. "I get that you want out, but it's not going to do you any favours if you drive your car up a tree. Come and stay at my place, I live in the middle of town, and you know the old saying – nothing is so well hidden as that which is in plain sight…"

"John, I…"

"It will be fine, they gave me a three-bedroom place in town. There's just me, my wife and my twin boys there, so there's a spare room. I occasionally get called out in the evening because I don't have backup here, so if I do, you'd be good company for my wife. I know we've just met, but you don't strike me as the kind of person who is going to take an axe to anyone."

"I guess…"

"I think it's the smart thing to do. Hide there, have some food, leave early tomorrow and not be so shaken up. In the meantime I can get to the bottom of what's going on and you are no doubt going to want to file a report on this mess, aren't you?"

"Do you think it will do any good? I don't think it was anyone in this town that would have trashed the place. The local football team looks after the garden and they are hardly going to vandalise the house of someone who helps buy their uniforms each year. Have a party in it, sure, but not just walk in and break stuff."

"I can't make you file a report, and it's less work for me if you don't, but I'd at least like to keep an eye on the place and make sure it doesn't get systematically destroyed when you're not in it."

"John, as far as I'm concerned you can have the keys to the place, I didn't want to come back here today and I'm not overly enthusiastic about coming back in the future."

"Let's talk about what happens next, later. Get your car and drive it to the back lot of the bar on Smithson, then walk through the alley to the front of the building, I'll be waiting there."

"Why all the cloak-and-dagger stuff?"

"Well," John looked a little sheepish "It's kind of fun, for me at least, nothing interesting happens around here, apart from a low key bar fight or some local farmer complaining that some young folk have been tipping his cows over in the middle of the night. This is the closest thing to police work I've had to do in ages."

I smiled, he was one of the good guys it seemed.

"Alright then, it's settled. We've got a plan…"

"Should we synchronise watches," I said, good naturedly, the humour laying a cool filter over the anger before.

"Yes, we should," John said, his face deadpan serious for about five seconds until the corners of his mouth wrinkled and gave way to a hearty giggle.

"You going to be okay here if I leave now? I'm going to let my wife know about our plans, and then pop out to McKinnon's farm, apparently he has some cow-tipping issues. I told you it wasn't that interesting around here."

I nodded and said that I'd be fine.

"I'll be at the pickup point in one hour, see you there," and he left, whistling the theme to mission impossible.

*****

It wasn't far into town, and with an hour up my sleeve I decided to do a little cleaning up. More for Her sake than mine. Intellectually I knew that this probably wasn't going to be the last time I came here; even if I sold the place, I'd still have to come back to supervise the emptying it of its previous life.

The idea of that felt both liberating, and very final. I spent twenty minutes just putting things back in their place. It appeared that whoever was in here was looking for something specific. I suspect the thing was in my satchel – my technological invisible cloaks, as it were.

I poured a glass of tonic – sniffing it first and then beginning with a small sip to make sure that I hadn't set another alcoholic trap in my stupor the night before.

Then sent a text to Bammer.

*'Local police concerned about license plate. Please advise.'*

Almost immediately a reply came.

*'Already flagged and resolved, will look like an error on his behalf, have added a deformation bug to the file.'*

*'I'm not liking this sneakiness B. AND someone was here this AM. Trashed the place. I was out.'*

*'You need to leave. Right now.'*

*'Doing that, have a safe house for the night, leave tomorrow.'*

*'Stop fucking texting and get in your car, they are coming for you. Leave NOW.'*

The urgency in Bam's text shook me, so I stuffed the last things into my bag, jammed my phone with my laptop into the satchel, and paused to unzip what I had begun to call 'the gun pocket'. I took one last look around and, seeing the evidence of the violence the intruder had used, reopened the satchel.

I took the gun out and loaded the magazine, which in turn slid into place with a solid and satisfying click. Tucking the gun back into its pocket, I felt it was past time to go.

The door closed and locked and screen door jiggled in to place, I turned toward the back yard.

There was something hanging from the hammock frame. I approached and gently put my hand into the gun pocket and felt the grip, cold and oddly calming as I drew it out of its new holster.

The note was hand-written in red ink and hung on the hook part of the frame like a carcass in an abattoir. Hanging. Gently moving in the very light breeze. I ripped at it, tearing it from its terrible resting place.

It had one sentence written on it.

"She has already been forgotten, she is nothing, as are we all."

I looked around and found that the once benign surroundings of the yard had become as threatening as any forest described by The Brothers Grimm. Every shadow hid violence, every move of leaf or bush was a terror waiting to be unleashed.

Walking purposefully to my car, I nonchalantly opened the passenger side and threw my bags in, then sidled around the driver's side. If I was being watched, I wasn't going to give them the pleasure of thinking they had already won.

"Fuck. You." I said as I got in the car, and shut the door, the locks making their electronic buzz as I hit the 'lock all doors' button.

"Fuck you," I said again, then started the car and drove off toward town.

# 14.

John was waiting exactly where he said he would be.

Barely breaking stride, I moved out of the alley and walked straight toward the car. John indicated that I should sit in the front, so I moved to that door and got in.

"Figured it'd be better for you to sit up here for two reasons," he said, indicating and then pulling into the street. "One: That seat back there is uncomfortable at the best of times, and two: people won't look so hard if you sit in the front. Sit in the back and it would be all over town by sundown that I had arrested somebody and was dragging them to the cooler," he said with a grin.

"Gotta love small towns," I replied, turning to look at the backseat of the police car. It did indeed look singularly uncomfortable; hard plastic with a large cutout area at junction of seat and back – presumably to allow people wearing handcuffs the ability to sit with their hands behind them.

"Do many people have to ride in the back?" I asked, returning my attention to the front.

"Not many, most of the time the guys that get put in the drunk-tank either turn themselves in for fear of going home late to their wives, or their friends drive them over. It's just the way it's done here," he said, that rueful smile playing on his lips again.

John's house was just perfect. The garden was well tended and, typical of many homes in the area, had a driveway that led down the side of the property to a free-standing garage. People in the beach town didn't often use their garages to store their cars though. Generally such a large part of their real estate was given over to storage of old things like boxes of read books, and things so very important that the home owner couldn't bear to throw them out, but not so important that they can't be allowed to rot in the quiet, still, and moist air of the structure out back.

He parked in front of the tilt-a-door and killed the engine.

We were both just getting out of the car when the door leading from the veranda to the house banged shut. John's wife paused on the top step, then bustled down the remaining couple of stairs toward the car.

With a warm smile and a hug, she greeted her husband and then me. Herding us inside, she directed us to the kitchen table, a fresh pot of coffee sitting on a cork mat, and a plate of biscuits which she implored us to try, "…while they are still warm, and before the boys get here."

'The boys' were twins, "exactly seven years and ninety-four days old," James and David announced, in stereo, before throwing themselves bodily at the plate of biscuits.

"You had better grab another one for yourself, those two are like cookie-piranhas, they could skeletonise a cake shop in a little under five minutes if left unattended."

The boys both looked up, crumbs dropping from the corners of their mouths, pausing their assault on the baked goods to look at everyone else in the room in turn, then ploughed right back in to the food.

"Your room is just down the hall there, second door on the right, it's right next to these two monsters but they are pretty quiet at night, thankfully," John's wife, Margaret, said as she ruffled the hair of her sons.

Both boys moved as one, the timing impeccable, to swat at their mothers hands. "Stop touching our hair," James said, speaking for both of them.

"We hate it when you do that, HATE it," chimed in David.

I smothered a smirk by looking into my satchel, and realised, uncomfortably, that the gun was still in the loose pocket on the outside of the satchel. Cursing myself for not placing it back in its hidden pocket during the haste of leaving the beach house, I clamped my hand over the protruding grip, hoping I hadn't created more trouble due to my laziness.

Margaret saw the weapon as well, and without any obvious reaction turned to her boys and said, "You two should take that plate into the lounge room, isn't that show you love so much on soon?"

"That sounds like code for grownup talk to me," said David.

"Sounds like we are allowed to watch TV to me," added James.

They left the room.

"I'm really sorry, I'm not used to carrying a g…," I began, fearful that I had already soured this relationship.

"It's fine", said Margaret, looking over to see John coming back from the bathroom,

"There are always those things in the house, I just don't want the boys to know where they are, they're responsible enough for their age, but boys will be boys," she had said 'those things' while looking toward the lounge to ensure the little men were out of earshot.

"I'll keep it hidden away, I promise," I said, feeling very much relieved.

*****

Margaret set about cooking dinner and I pitched in to help, although I suspect that I was getting in the way as much as being helpful. Margaret didn't seem to mind. John had to go out on a call but returned within the hour. (Turns out the guy at the hardware store had taken offence at the neighbouring butcher's shop for suggesting the butcher's customers should just park in the couple of places allocated for the hardware store. It was an ongoing feud and one that would probably never be settled. The fact that both the business owners were brothers seemed to have no bearing on the subject.)

No more callouts plagued the officer for the afternoon, so he 'clocked out' at six o'clock and immediately went to the fridge for a beer.

"Want one?" he asked.

"Don't you two go and ruin your appetites with a gallon of beer now," said Margaret.

"Honey, it's just one beer and besides, when have I ever left anything behind that you have cooked? Huh?" said John, putting his arm around his wife's shoulder and kissing her on the side of the head, while carrying two cans of beer in his free hand.

She pushed him away playfully and John came over to the table and sat across from me, opening and placing a can in front of me.

"Thanks."

"No problem, I'd hate to drink alone," said John.

"You are kidding, right?" said Margaret over her shoulder.

"While I went out on that call I popped back by the station, to see whether Emma had found anything."

"Emma?"

"She's the administrative girl at the station, she does the work of three people. Really hard on her at the moment without the extra police officer here."

"Didn't see her this morning."

"No she works afternoon shift, three days a week, and I handle the desk, makes it a little easier on her."

I nodded, "Makes sense."

"So, I went in to see what she found with your car, and it seems to be all sorted out. Must have been how I added the info or something, haven't seen anything like it before. But I guess there is a first time for everything." He took a swig of his beer.

"I didn't think there'd be a problem," I said, trying to end the subject as fast as I could. Even if the situation was clear, the reality is that I didn't think that it would stand up to any kind of close scrutiny.

Thankfully a noise from the front room interrupted our conversation. The twins had had an argument and had decided to duke it out as only brothers can. John got up and went to see what was going on, Margaret took that as her cue to take a break from cooking, pulled an opened bottle of chardonnay from the refrigerator, and poured herself a large glass.

"They're our life, they really are, but they are almost the same person, and when they get angry…"

"Boys will be boys, didn't you say that?"

"Yes, and twin boys create double the headaches! Any wonder I need wine in the evenings."

Margaret laughed and offered me a glass which I declined, so without asking she went to the refrigerator, retrieved a can of beer and placed it, opened, in front of me.

John returned, a sullen looking boy either side of him.

"What do you have to say for yourselves?" he asked, as he looked straight at me, and allowed a brief wink.

"We're sorry," they said, in precise timing and tone.

"What are you sorry for?" said John.

Both boys shuffled their feet, and said, "We're sorry for knocking the table over and spilling the rest of the biscuits."

"But…," said one of them.

"It's not our fault really."

"Oh no?" I said.

"No… if there was an even number of cookies on the plate we wouldn't have had to fight over the last one. There's been two of us for a while now, so it's not like it's a surprise we need even numbers."

Everyone laughed. Margaret even managed to spray a little chardonnay with the unexpected force of her laughter. The boys looked at the adults, confused at the mirth, and unsure if that meant they were still in trouble or not.

John returned to his seat and picked up his beer while failing dismally at trying to regain some semblance of fatherly order.

The boys looked around again and decided it would be in their best interests to leave while the going was good.

Everyone pretended not to see them go.

It was the kind of family that She and I could only have dreamed of having. I settled in to another can of beer, chatting amiably with the two adults. Our conversation punctuated now and then by the noise and voices of the young ones as they rumbled and argued before, and then during dinner.

I tried to help Margaret clean up after the meal, but every attempt was waved away. "Please, you're a guest. If you don't like it, I'm happy to stand back and let you clean up if ever we are at your house." she said.

Accepting defeat, I went out on to the back porch and sat on the stair below the one John was sitting on.

"I gave up smoking when the boys were born and I don't miss it. But I still like to be outside after dinner. Some strange habit."

I had nothing to add, so we sat in comfortable silence.

"You looked rattled when you walked up to the car in town today," he said.

I told him about the note. I told him part of what was suggested by Bammer without naming her or giving details. I told him I was worried that whatever the hell was going on was big. Bigger than me.

I told him how much I loved Her, and that being around his family was bittersweet. I told him I loved his kids, and that I had hoped that I could dream a life where She was alive and we had children like his. "But I'd like one of each, not that there is anything wrong with two boys."

"Have you been inside that house for the last few hours? Everything is wrong with having two identical boys," he said, laughing.

Margaret came out and handed us both another beer, and sat in the chair near the door with a glass of wine for herself, lighting a cigarette.

I looked at her, then to him, without a prompt he said, "I gave up smoking, but a certain someone was back on them the minute the children gave up on her boobs," he threw a twig from one of the bushes that encroached on the stair, it landed in Margaret's lap.

"I don't smoke in front of them and I only have a couple a day you big grump," she said and lobbed the twig back at her husband, then stuck out her tongue.

"They'll…" he began and she finished, affecting a reasonable approximation of John's tone of voice "…kill you in the end, I gave up you know. Best thing I ever did."

\*\*\*\*\*

52 hours later, she was dead, along with her husband, and both their children.

Murder-suicide they said, although the initial report noted that John, the alleged perpetrator, had been found with defensive wounds and was lying in a position that suggested that he had been protecting his family. Margaret had been shot twice at close range, three times for James, just once for David. John had been shot seven times.

Seven times is a pretty definite act of self-criticism.

The record, of course, was altered for posterity, a bug was placed almost immediately after the case was closed. Even eyewitness accounts of John with an unknown stranger driving through town were soon erased.

Look at the file now, and all the questionable evidence has gone. What is left is a horrid insult to a good man and his beautiful family.

# 15.

We got hold of the police report early. Bammer and I. Bammer had flagged the police department at the beach in her deeper than deep tunnel to the Central Data.

We came to call anything we got through that tunnel as coming from 'Central Data', like Central Data was its own country, and we, its two consumers, were its only citizens.

The banality of some of the stuff we were mining out of it meant that the mysterious other end of the tunnel was as much like the pizza store around the corner. If we needed to feast on delicious and junky information, we got it hot and fresh from Central Data.

Bammer installed a new code string to the matrix of information that was mounting up on the small server we shared. It had taken her a while to work the kinks out but it sped up our progress immensely with regard to the problems that come from a lot of data, and not a lot of time or human hours to sift through it. With this new string we were able to grasp at the shadowy patterns as they were forming; meaning we could get into the flow of data as it happened - while all the lights were on, so to speak – rather than showing up late to the party because we hadn't known until the last minute what was happening.

Before Bammer's new code, we had blundered through as best we could and made pretty good progress, but lacked subtlety in our search methods.

Every time we came close to something we felt was significant, the game would change. Not just a redirection or false thread, the change was deeper than that: it was almost as if whoever was moulding the data knew it was being watched, and so covered it. Hid it. Threw their arms over it to so that people passing by wouldn't see what they were doing to the delicate flesh of collected information.

With this new research power, we could find anything. Change anything. We had access to the cunts and crematoriums of the world. We could track people from birth to death. All from a shitty motel on a secondary road to nowhere.

We both had our own reasons to keep sifting through the data. For me, it was trying to find Her killer, with a side order of finding the murderer of John and his family. For Bammer it was the cut and thrust of finding ways to shore up the tunnel. Our connection was attacked daily - Bammer took care of it. Sometimes it was a tweak, other times it meant a 30 hour stint plugging holes that appeared in our safety zone.

She'd do it.

And then sleep.

I knew what I was doing it for, but her? At that moment I was certain most of her motivation was to avoid any situation where she would have to look in the mirror.

We settled into a solid team groove about one year after I'd left the beach for the last time. Bammer was all about the tech. I was all about research.

I understood the mechanics of erasure, to some degree, but I couldn't understand the motivation behind it. As a result, I really couldn't understand why She had become the victim of it.

*****

Bammer came to me with a printout one morning, looking ragged. I suspected she had been up most of the night.

"What's this?" I asked, as she handed over a large file.

"THAT is a pattern schedule. That is about as close as we have gotten to a key to this lock," she said as she plunked down onto the bed.

"And what am I to do with it?"

"You keep on telling me how you 'research'" she said, adding the air quotes, "so here's some 'research' for you to get your teeth in to."

"Right, more pawing through random online chat-rooms and forums for me then."

"You'll also be pleased to know that the tunnel now ports directly past all the international filters."

"What do you mean?"

"I mean that each country has its own set of filters, put in place to ensure its citizens are only privy to the information that that country deems useful and controllable. The US, for instance, represents only thirteen percent of internet traffic, but has a filter set in place. So that means regular citizens only see five percent of what is actually out there. Our tunnel now has access to every page that is released to the weird wide web."

"Wow."

"Thought you'd like it. Happy hunting."

Having unfettered access to all of the world's information didn't at first look much different to what I had been used to. To be fair though, I had built up a pretty strong callous when it came to information coming out of the screen. Porn was still porn, whackos were whackos. Car companies still jammed advertising in the middle of whatever I was reading to invite me to test-drive their new car. So at first it was familiar territory, if somewhat louder and more frequent.

It took about a week of solid use before I noticed a more subtle change, or at least recognising that there was more 'stuff' coming my way than usual. Websites previously on the periphery of the criminal and insane became the anchor points to safety. Lifelines back into the light of reasonable thought. They sat on the edge of the light, beyond which was a swirling, hideous pit of collective human conscious. There was no law, no arbiter and, like some Tolkien-esque spectre, I found myself tentatively feeling my way about. Even within the alleged anonymity of Bammer's tunnel, the feeling of having your life stripped bare was palpable.

At first, my attempts to fit in were as successful as a city kid pulling on a cowboy hat and trying to blend in at a rodeo.

My comments on people's sites stank of outsider. My questions were ridiculed, and I was told to go back to my mass-consumption sites and community-service info-tainment portals. I was told it was dangerous in these new and darkened sites, and that I was trying to invade. And that I would be dealt with.

This was familiar territory: I'd been in flame wars in online forums for years. My early attempts to make contact in this new project, though, were met with a whole different level of aggression and support by other posters. The kind that had me getting up to look out the window, half expecting to see someone there. Watching. Coming for me.

I found very quickly that I was relegated to simply lurking in sites that I felt would lead somewhere. I had to wait, tentatively running out of the dark to leave a couple of words in the centre of the forum to appease the moderators. Hoping that I would be invited into a new circle. Allowed as an apprentice or page to the court. Often seen, occasionally acknowledged.

It took months before I had been elevated to a level that, while still not inner sanctum, at least meant I had a voice and a little influence.

The sites I trudged through the dark to visit required that I had friends, for both access and protection. Using my created persona I tried to collect contacts and allies. Not specifically people that would know anything about Her, but people who could open doors I suspected would lead me closer to the those who would.

Information was hard to come by, even with the connections I had nurtured. So deep was I into the data web, that the pages often didn't link to each other - they were just lists of data, and the only way they could be accessed was if someone offered the physical address of the page. Some of those addresses were heavily encrypted and up to one hundred and fifty characters long, and often good only for a day or two. Many were good for an hour.

Frustrating and long, I knew I just had to wait it out. If I pushed even a little too much, the half-lit faces fled and I would be left alone, sometimes for days at a time.

The cat-and-mouse strategy seemed to bear fruit, but the slowness involved in chipping away took time, and I found myself in front of the computer for twenty hours at a stretch. I still ran up to an hour a day. A routine I would keep up, nap-eat-run for days at a time; then crash and sleep, dreaming of black screens. All the time Her face looked back, just out of reach, concealed by the data.

# 16.

Perhaps after a month from when Bammer supplied me the pattern schedule, I realised that presenting myself on the forums as being the loved one of a victim returned very little other than occasional frustrated sympathy. Although, from time to time the sympathetic voices were drowned out by some cruel taunting from roving flamers looking to start a fight – usually by suggesting that they knew who did it. Sometimes offering up exact information of venues and dates, names of work friends. As a result, the person being assaulted would disappear for a few days, or a couple of weeks, before hopeless desperation drew them back to the threads.

My moment came when I offered a photo of the mark that was left on Her. The traffic to that post exploded, initially from victims' friends saying they had seen the same mark either amongst the person's things, on a window, in one case in lipstick on a mirror – the thread and the site that it was on disappeared in less than 15 minutes.

Other threads that mentioned the demise of the previous forum and the poster who added an unusual symbol were also slammed shut.

The decision to send that photo cost me four weeks work, but taught me a lesson. I needed to start again, that was certain. I needed to have no connection to Her.

*****

Search for anything and a rhythm forms, the tendrils of each search thread like capillaries, alive with potential information. If the researcher is only a little conscientious and keeps their wits about them, paths that could be overlooked become as important as those that seem obvious to follow. Such potential paths become landmarks to be revisited.

Blundering into a new data funnel without heed or respect can have dire research consequences; at best the blunder can be covered up by staying still and not poking the meat of what is inside.

Worse is to have the funnel slam shut, denying access, and forcing the researcher to walk back over paths to new links and detours to try again to acquire the keys to the corridor they were evicted from.

Worse still, the system of research can implode, causing a chain reaction of server routes and webpage name changes, leaving the researcher isolated and alone.

It took some time, but as I became a new citizen of the webs both deep and dark, and the complex hierarchy of space and data, I began to regard such spaces as real and solid as cities: resilient, constantly renewing and fortifying and cleaning up themselves while archiving yesterday's structures should they ever need to be used again.

In an attempt to find likeminded people I followed paths no matter how tenuously they related to what I was searching for. Perhaps other people were searching for murdered loved ones, although more and more I found myself interchanging the term murdered with erased, until they meant one and the same thing when used in the correct context.

After the initial failure, I decided to change my plan. In my heart I knew that in order to stay true to Her I needed to leave Her completely anonymous during the process of finding her again. My new approach was to actively try to become part of the group that killed her, not part of the group who have had loved ones killed.

I returned to the search, the threads offering more now because I wasn't protecting Her from scrutiny.

It was in this way that I found the way to The Movement.

# 17.

"B, I have to go away for at least a couple of weeks. Maybe a month or more. Will this tunnel stay intact no matter where I am?" I asked as we shared some rare TV time and a bottle of wine.

"Where are you going?" she asked, concern evident in her voice.

"I'd rather not discuss that," I said. "You'll know where I am of course, because you'll no doubt track my passport movement. I'm fine with that, there needs to be an anchor, and at least you'll know where to send the search party if I go all incommunicado." I was trying to lighten the situation, and realised at once I was unsuccessful.

"So that's it?" she said.

I realised there was a little more at stake even thou I would be continuing our work, albeit at another location.

"Our relationship is 95% data based anyway, what difference would it make if that data came from another continent?"

"That's not what I meant," she said.

"What did you mean then?"

"Oh, nothing. I've just got so used to you being here. I've not been this well in years. You've been here for months, and yes, sometimes there's been a week without seeing you, but just knowing you were only a couple of hundred footsteps from where I sat has been comforting." She took a large swig of her wine.

I realised that in all this, for all her weirdness, I was being pretty cavalier by simply announcing that I was going to go after all these months. I had grown accustomed to her being around as well, even if it was in some weird twilight world of TV re-runs and indulging in Bammer's extraordinary selection of cheap wines.

"I'm sorry Bam, I should have put it more kindly…"

"It is what it is," she said, sullenly.

"No, it's more than what it appears to be. You helped me and sheltered me and kept me safe, I am very grateful for that. I should probably show more gratitude than I do. I'm just so focussed, so when this invitation that I've been trying to secure came up, I didn't even draw breath. I'm in the zone is all." I leant over and brushed a strand of hair away from her forehead.

Bam was looking a little flushed.

"I'm sorry, I should think more about you," I said.

"No, I'm just too highly strung; you do what you have to do. Yes, I can track your general movements, and yes, you are right not to give me specifics. We're safe here, but it would be foolish to think that no-one will work out where we are." she said and adjusted her glasses. Her arm, while heavily scarred showed no new marks.

She continued, "When are you hoping get away?"

"Ten days from now is the goal. I have to set up a story line for the forums that will help explain why I'll be sporadic in the time and frequency of posts while I'm away. I'll just have to make up something."

"I'll clean your passport, and bug the system so you'll be untrackable. Just don't get drunk on the plane. Also, let me know if you need news items added to regional papers to back up any catastrophes you might decide to use as an alibi."

"I'm going to keep it pretty low key, but if I think of anything I'll let you know. Maybe an aunt's obituary might be in order," I said.

"Birthday would be easier, a death notice can be cross-checked with a death certificate, and that gets a little tricky. I mean it can be done, but it's a lot of work for an alibi you might not even use," she replied.

"True. You are pretty good at this sneaky stuff aren't you?"

"You are such a sweet talker," said Bam, filling up her glass before scooting closer to me and putting her head on my shoulder. I put my free hand around her and she drew closer still, I leant and kissed her on her temple, my lips feeling the border where hair meets skin.

We stayed that way, as we did on these odd occasions, until well after midnight when Bam had got up and stretched her hand out to help me rise as well. We stood facing each other, so close I could smell the wine still on her lips, could feel her breath. She stepped into my arms only briefly, and for a second we held each other before she pushed closer again, our bodies in complete contact.

Then she was moving away, stumbling while moving toward the door.

"Good night," she said as she carefully opened the door and left.

*****

I saw Bam more in the week prior to me leaving than I had in the previous month. Usually, we had a loose agreement that on Friday or Saturday (rarely both) we would have dinner in my room, drink wine until we couldn't be bothered anymore and then she'd go. Although before the night I announced my departure for an undetermined amount of time, there hadn't been any awkwardness.

We had often sat on the floor upon a spare bedspread, folded so that its old quilting would pad our backsides from the aged, paper-thin carpet. Often we would sit wrapped in each other's arms. I had naïvely treated this time as two lost and lonely people taking comfort. Until the night when Bam stumbled out the door, I hadn't realised that for her this might be the closest thing to a relationship she had had for a long time.

In that week it seemed to become a nightly occurrence, and regardless of my misgivings about what this new level of contact meant, I didn't protest.

Figuring that the situation was obvious, I fooled myself into thinking that the level of our intimacy was manageable and was completely understood by both of us.

In that final week Bam took to wearing far more revealing attire than I had grown used to. When she found excuses to get up from our quilted carpet-camp I chose to ignore that she would move in just such a way that whatever part of her lower body she was electing to display wound up thrust in close proximity to me, and in direct eye line.

I chose indifference when on the second last night, dressed uncharacteristically in short skirt and tight shoe stringed singlet top, she moved from her place next to me and on hands and knees crawled over to the TV stand to retrieve that day's paper. Her legs, in full view, were still scarred of course, but no new additions had been made. She turned and crawled back, her breasts pushing the fabric forward, and so offering a more than tantalising view of clear white skin. Her arms mimicking the all but healed patina of her legs.

She looked directly at me as I was contemplating her anatomy, and I looked quickly away.

"You don't have to be bashful," she said, "They're just boobs after all." She plopped back to her spot, the shoulder strap of her top slipped and rested in the crease made where her arm leant against mine.

"I'm sorry, I was just… I don't know. You're Bam."

"What is that supposed to mean?" she asked.

"Well, I just don't see you in a sexual way. I don't think of anyone in a sexual way. Not since Her. I just don't think that being intimate would benefit either of us," I said.

"It's okay," she said quietly, "I wouldn't fuck me either."

"Don't do this Bam. Don't do this to yourself, and certainly don't implicate me and who I would and wouldn't fuck. I'm broken, and I don't know if I'll ever be put back together or even function at that level ever again."

"The old 'it's not you it's me' thing is it?"

"Bam…"

"It's okay," she said and moved away a little.

I put my arm around her and pulled at her to come back, she resisted at first and then relaxed.

"Who'd have thought it would be this hard to have a first time."

"More reason why it wouldn't be a good idea, Bam."

*****

She asked if she could stay, and sleep with me, "And I mean sleep," she added. "I didn't realise how much I was going to miss you, I mean I knew you were going to have to go sometime, but…"

Missing me was one thing, staying in my bed after the conversation we had earlier was likely to be awkward, but in truth I was going to miss her too. I'd miss the familiarity of her, and the comfort of knowing that she was around.

"Alright, but no funny business," I said, channelling my best stereotypical parental tone.

"I prooomise," she replied, with a saintly look on her face.

We pushed the beds together. I stripped down to my underwear and got in, me facing away from her side as she got undressed. It wasn't until she had got under the covers and snapped the lamps off that I realised she was naked. She snaked her arms around me and nuzzled into the back of my neck. Her breasts, pushing firmly into my back, nipples firm, and I felt myself easing backward into her embrace.

A hand traced my side, my neck, into my hair, then down my cheek stopping briefly at my collar bone…

"Bam. You have to stop it. This is not going to go anywhere." I said, voice cracking in my throat.

"Really? You seem to be enjoying it."

"Bam. BAM!" I said and moved out of bed, turning the lights on again.

Bam lay naked on the bed, the cover strewn around her.

"Bam, I said no and I meant it."

Her face went from a look of genuine surprise to steely cold. "Fine, it's probably better if I go then." She got up unselfconsciously and walked naked to the desk, where her clothes hung over the back of one of the chairs.

I said nothing as she dressed and left, closing the door firmly behind her.

No parting shot was levelled at me, and in some peculiar way it was that silence that worried me most.

# 18.

I didn't see her the following morning, my last full A.M. before I left the motel for the next part of my research assignment.

I was due to leave early the next day and hoped to catch up with Bammer sometime during the day to finalise some arrangements. Some were more mundane; the usual administrational stuff that is required before leaving, along with more serious affairs –like a new will I had drafted should I not return.

Lastly, I wanted to clear the air between us. I couldn't just leave and have her believe that I thought nothing of her. I wasn't in a position to commit to anything, but I wanted her to know that I cared about her and her safety.

I decided to go for a run in the hope that she might see my return and that would inspire her to make contact. To help this little plan along I sent her an email immediately before I left.

*"Bam, I'm going for a run, you want lunch when I get back? xx"*

Before I could even get out the door, my email notification sounded.

*"And I suppose you'd like your passport back, now that I have finished all this work on it, don't worry, you'll get it. Can't have you missing your plane now, can we?"*

I went for a run.

On my return my door was unlocked and lunch was waiting on the desk with a note. *"Waiting on a*

*couple of things to finalise with your travel stuff. I'll
come and see you at 6. B"*

I spent the afternoon relaxing, and even, for the
first time in a long time, started to read a book. I
really only logged in to the data tunnel to check that
there hadn't been any new and surprising tangents
on any of the forums. None arose, so by the time
Bam arrived at 5.55pm I was more than a little 'zen'
about things.

She knocked and then strode through the door,
closing it behind her. Bam was wearing almost
exactly what she wore the first time I saw her with
the lights on, different t-shirt maybe, but the jeans
and jacket looked the same.

Dramatically, Bam threw two large envelopes on
the bed, and without breaking stride walked over to
the desk and placed a bottle of wine there.

She didn't say hello, she just launched straight in
to a pre-operation-briefing that I suspect she had
rehearsed a couple of times before coming to the
room.

"…I went ahead and appropriated 10k in a
mixture of notes from your account. In addition to
that, you'll also find two cash cards that you can use
at most banks throughout the world. Each card has
an additional five thousand on them and I suggest
that if you need to use either of them that you draw
the full balance and then destroy the used card."

"Thanks Bam, I…"

"The other envelope contains your passport, and
a selection of travel documents that I thought you
might need. Because of your whole thing about

mystery, I've not activated the visas. Just text me as you are approaching whatever immigration desk you find yourself at and I'll make sure that it gets activated. Or, you can just go line up with the plebs, I don't give a fuck."

"Bam…"

"That wine there," she indicated the bottle on the desk, "is a going-away present. I've ordered some Thai food to be delivered in an hour or so. So I think that about rounds things out. Have a nice trip, I'll of course be here when or if you decide to return. Or I'll be dead because you've been clumsy and compromised the safety here, not that you should be too concerned I guess…"

"That's enough…"

"Is it?" she said, "Okay then, I'll be dismissed, have a good trip." She held out her hand to suggest we should shake on it so she could be going.

It was then that I saw the blood, dried and revealed as she stretched her hand forward, her jacket creeping up her arm a little.

"Bam, what the fuck is that? What have you been doing?"

She clasped her left hand down and over her right wrist in an attempt to smooth the sleeve and cover this new evidence of abuse.

She moved away and made to turn for the door, but not fast enough. Her shame made her limp and disoriented. I easily passed her and blocked the only exit.

"Bam, what have you done?"

She was already crying. Shaking her head. Not wanting to make whatever was underneath the jacket real. Her legs began to buckle, the business-like exterior of a minute ago, gone.

I grabbed at her as she sagged and she flinched before letting me ease her back to sit on the edge of the bed.

She was crying. Heavy sobs that came from some deep pit of sorrow spewed from her mouth.

Kneeling down in front of her I caught both her hands in mine, "Take your jacket off B."

"No," she said, snot dangling from her nose.

"Bam, you are going to take that jacket off."

"Now you want to undress me. Last week all I wanted was for you to ask me to take my clothes off, and now, after I've been sick and cut holes in my arms, now you want me to undress."

"Just your jacket, B. Let me help you."

Her left arm was sliced lightly but her right had five cuts, deep lacerations held together with butterfly plasters, and still weeping considerably.

"When did you do this?"

"Last night."

"Why?"

"I needed to know."

"You needed to know what?"

"Why you weren't attracted to me. Why we seem to get only so far before you freeze over. I needed to know what was so hideous that you wouldn't want me. "

"Jesus, Bam."

"… so I thought I was strong enough to look in the mirror, and I was okay at first," she said, her breath stammering, wiping her nose on a tissue I had handed her. "I thought I could do it, find the answer, and I was doing well, HAVE been doing well all these months. Then I fell apart because it is pointless lying to myself. It's no wonder you have no interest in me, I am just… vile."

I had no answer, I tried to tell her that for me her scars had disappeared long ago, that this was entirely an evil thought process that manifested itself in her own head, but she was exhausted and simply lay back on the bed and slept.

I watched over her while she dozed, and then gently roused her when the food came. She sat up for a while and said that she should probably eat something, so we split the food, passing the takeaway containers to each other periodically, as we sipped wine and sat on the floor in front of the TV.

When the alarm went off at 5am, she was gone. Bam had left sometime between us dozing off in each other's arms and the screech of the motel-issue alarm clock.

I was fearful that she had gone to do herself more harm, but five minutes later, as I was still getting the stiffness from my limbs, a knock, a quiet entry, and the smell of freshly brewed coffee allayed some of my concerns.

# 19.

I had never been to Heathrow Airport before, but it lived up to its reputation. Large, bustling and staffed with immigration officials that either really take their job and the nation's security to heart or realised that for all the jobs that they had the skill set for, 'immigration officer' was the one that would let them wield the most power. All while offering the unique opportunity to make people feel vulnerable, confused and somehow indebted that they should be allowed through the gate they presided upon.

I'd flown business class. I hadn't set out to, even though (because of Her insurance bequest) I certainly had the money. Still, habit meant that when I booked my flight I had forgotten that I could afford to fly in any seat other than economy, so was pleasantly surprised when I was immediately upgraded to business class. The apologetic person at the check-in desk said that it was the best he could do as all of first class had been booked by a Middle Eastern family.

"But, if you'd like to wait four hours for the next flight, I can place you in first class, and write you a hotel voucher so you can go and rest in the meantime," the check-in guy had said.

"No, truly, it's fine. Business class is fine. Please don't worry about it," I replied, making a real effort to not sound like the entitled fools that he no doubt had to regularly deal with.

"Thank you, I...I really appreciate your understanding."

It seems that in Bam's cleaning and realigning of my travel documents, she had also managed to fill my frequent flyer account with travel miles, and had not just added me to the airline's membership program, but made sure I was upgraded to the highest possible level.

I got the feeling that Heads of State had fewer privileges than my new flight status offered.

The business seat was fine, as business class seats often are. However, in what was probably a gesture of good-will, the seat next to me was free – lest I be disturbed by some undesirable riffraff, I guess.

The real benefit to Bam's meddling became apparent as I was approaching the immigration gates at Heathrow, where it would be a coin toss as to whether the attendant was going to be having a good day or a bad one. Even with my preferred customer gate pass, it was with some trepidation that I approached the immigration officer.

Clearly, I hadn't realised the level of pass that the steward had given me. A smile, a stamp, and a separate corridor that came out at the baggage collection, where I found my bags already loaded on to a trolley. As I approached, I was greeted by a porter, who smiled nervously and then led me to another corridor entirely bypassing baggage inspection.

I had travelled enough to know that this was definitely something I could get used to.

*****

London was the starting point for The Movement, and so I wasn't surprised that the invitation had led me to that famous and fabulous city. All I knew about the group was pieced together over the weeks and months spent hunkered over the machine at the motel.

The Movement was led by a core group of people who called themselves 'The Analysts', and had its roots in the discussion of Big Brother type concerns.

It worked as a kind of collective, but apart from a loose acceptance that the longer someone was involved in the group, the more their opinions would be listened to, the membership was at best, haphazard. The result of this loose membership meant that, at least at the beginning, The Movement was hardly a world-shaking underground cult.

In the early days, the information regarding the meeting places was heavily encoded and often found in independent magazines or mainstream classified advertisements in newspapers. Sometimes the directions given in the messages were obvious once the referring words were found. Other times the notification only served to start a kind of treasure hunt, each step offering a new clue to a trail that ultimately ended in the back room of a house, or arty café where beer was served in pints and the only coffee available came in two varieties - filtered, or espresso.

While not entirely forbidden to directly help others in finding these events, it was most certainly frowned upon. The theory being that only the strongest and sharpest minds should find their way to these microcosms of the intellectual elite. The romantic nature and difficulty of securing information drew many toward the fledgling cult purely because of its exclusivity. Many of the early members were there because they could spend the rest of their dreary week with a secret, smug feeling that they didn't have to share with their interminable workmates and school colleagues.

A high percentage of those early members, particularly those that could decipher the really complex *Analyst* codes were probably the kind of people that, if not shunned, were on the outer fringe of society in their stagnant real-lives.

No one gave any consideration to the concept that The Movement could one day be considered a cult, even though a few more clear-thinking members observed that many of their fellow attendees tended to the fanatic. The common ground for many was the deep-seated, and for the most part, misguided, belief that in some small way they might be able to wield actual power, or maybe even change the world.

They gave the fledgling cult their time and The Movement gave them something many had never had before: respect and credibility. Even if that hard-won currency was limited to trading within a secretive group.

The early members thrived on it.

The analysts came together in additional backroom meetings, collating and debriefing the discussions they had had in more open meetings.

Many of the contributors, of course, were members of as many as half a dozen clandestine and some not so secretive groups. They came to meetings with reports of talks held in these other gatherings, to be added to the discussion forum of The Movement, the distillation of that information again ending up with The Analysts.

The intentions were good; the vibe of the gatherings was potent and dripping with a desire to fight the coming tide.

That tide was one of mass control, imposed by governments and deployed via media. It was also the beginning of the digital age, a situation that accelerated the fervour of those who thought they were in the know.

When news of a new communication system called 'Internet' was beginning to filter into the discussions it was, at first, heralded by The Movement as a way that would allow more input into the meetings. Members could report in from farther afield, and for the most part in the early years this new and exciting Internet thing did offer a very useful contribution system.

The online presence started out in a text-based relay chat room environment with rotating and encoded passwords to keep the spirit of intellect and secrecy alive. With the ability to work and associate remotely, the 90's saw the core of the rank and file members decentralised, only gathering now and then for festivities and end-of-year meet ups.

The Analysts, though, maintained a schedule of personal contact to decipher the information - now immense in scale - in an effort of almost monastic undertaking.

By the year 2005, The Movement was balanced on a tightrope – one side encouraging the use of the Internet and the now sophisticated community system. On the other side, the realisation that the tools employed in using the World Wide Web were also the embodiment of the very concept they had rallied against in the first place.

Both The Movement and the Internet had become independently huge, and inextricably linked. The group had political power and used the Internet as mechanism to rally the members. The Movement was also self-funded and at the forefront of search-engine-marketing, the funds pushed back into a system that conducted more research on the profitability of online commerce. The surplus of funds each year went toward those higher up in the hierarchy. All members knew that if they were promoted to Analyst there would be a significant salary sent their way. Not enough to buy million dollar cars, but more than enough to live comfortably. The senior Analysts earned even more, some offering no more than half a dozen mumbled comments per meeting, but admired for the quality and the insight those few words held.

Though, like all massive para-political organisations, there were factions within factions amongst The Movement's structure. Individually, many members were doing their best to climb the ladder, and so modified the information that they collated to better serve their position. The regular members had developed their own factionalism, with Left Movement vs. Right Movement groups regularly indulging in long and protracted debates and arguments, sometimes resulting in aggressive viral attacks and an occasional blowing up of a car that required the intervention of the High Analyst Board.

Despite such divisions, The Movement controlled any damage caused by infighting and steered its members to do its bidding – punishing those that fell foul of the doctrines. Even with this tenuous governance in place, murders were committed and entire lives shattered by operatives meddling with accounts and public records.

In short, The Movement had become everything it had rallied against in the backrooms of bars and cafés of 1989.

A faction called the Central Movement released a document outlining this very problem and expressing their disillusionment at the behaviour of some of the other sub groups and many of those in the Analyst tiers.

The group had combed through every corner of the network in order to put together the most comprehensive list of members ever held in one database. The ensuing document was sent to all of the addresses that could be found, and held views critical of how The Movement had lost its way and how it had in many cases helped develop the very mechanisms of mass media and control that it had once feared. To illustrate the point, they appended the document with a trace on one person, listing everything about the individual that was available. From the obvious information like birth and marriage records, to the more intricate and intimate details of their lives. Supermarket purchases, holidays taken, the list was comprehensive and more than a little disquieting.

The Document ended with an entire rundown of the technologies involved in gaining the information and how they could all be attributed to The Movement.

Within a week, The Movement went into meltdown, and lost a large percentage of members. Those in the Central Movement were forced into hiding, as threats of the most extreme kinds of violence were levelled at them. Analyst panels were disbanded, mistrustful of each other and trying to place blame regarding who would offer up such information to the Central Group.

Unexpectedly, The Movement received support from another small but growing splinter group - a quasi-religious order known as The Cult. This new group worked at eradicating people's lives so that they could leave this mortal plane unfettered and unhindered by the ties that held them to earth.

Some could feel a sense of connectedness to what The Cult was suggesting, others simply joined because they felt so disillusioned by the original Movement and what they had unwittingly done in its name, that they felt they could absolve themselves by joining the Cult, even if only to feel part of something.

For many, joining this new incarnation of The Movement was a spiritual awakening that that took their current beliefs, shaken as those beliefs were, and added an element higher-purpose to them. They spoke loudly that it is true and proven that everything is the contrivance of man and therefore nothing is the will of God.

The theory was simple enough: After death, in order for the soul to ascend to an afterlife the deceased needed to be forgotten by those left behind. Furthermore, any illustrative memory would prolong the time the soul was bound to the earth. A simple enough theory to give breath to, certainly, but it soon became an increasingly complex belief system to set rules for.

As a religion, it was in itself an experiment in compressed evolution.

What did illustrative memory mean? Was it enough to leave no photographs or pictorial evidence? Or, if the Document produced by the Central Group was true, could the data contained in a person's file - growing ever more intricate as data collation improved – could that data illustrate the person enough to have them recognised at a personal level by a complete stranger?

It took a year or so after the founding of The Cult for the first bible-esque book to be released. It was small and covered the fundamental aspects of what earthly connection meant. It also allowed and encouraged interpretation, the Cult's many appointed (and well-paid) archive disciples pawing over potential additions and omissions.

Edition II was released a year later and it said, in language that smacked of some embellishment, that the soul is bound here on earth while there is cohesive evidence to support its previous existence and, as the natural state is to be forgotten, the disciples were to do their best to cover their tracks in order to expedite their transitions when it was their turn to leave this earthly form.

It also purported that, if the existential footprint were to be made less, the process of being forgotten by loved ones and acquaintances should last only a generation and the soul would be left to wander and assist, Angel like, in the lives of those closest to them. As the people with recallable memory died, the soul would finally be released, its place taken by the newly deceased, who in turn would have to wait until all that remembered them died, and so the process wore on. All of that information could be found in The Book under the heading 'The Natural Way'.

Almost immediately, Cult members previously involved in programming and digital attacks started writing virus software that would systematically track down every last piece of a person's identifying information and then make the trail of the individual too muddled to be a cohesive dossier, thus dispersing the digital data memory.

A similar process was used to alter photographs enough so that the memory of the subject was changed, and therefore the memory of those left behind also changed, but passively, over a protracted period of time.

Much discussion on the Cult forums was made of this last effort regarding the subject of remaining human memory, with some testifying that they looked forward to spending time benignly watching over their loved ones and assisting their progress in life if they could.

Others took a different approach and purposely sought out remote places of the earth to exist in, leaving no trace behind, and having little, if anything, to do with the outside world.

More still opted to be anonymous in plain sight, living in the heart of thriving cities, taking the opinion that it is easy to remember a face of someone found on a lonely hill-top, but almost impossible to remember a person, let alone have a meaningful interaction with them, when their face is one of a thousand seen in a day.

A smaller group set themselves up as the Erasure faction – a group that the Cult only partially supported. They were a small but talented group that, for a fee, would erase the lives of people. Their clients included those that had lost loved ones and felt the need to assist them in passing on or, as some kind of memorial, just erased parts of the departed's lives as a token of love. Others still were wealthy people with terminal illnesses and little desire to wait around, and wanted to pay large sums to have themselves eradicated from the history books, so when it was their time they could behave as selfishly in the afterlife as they did in their living, breathing existence. Essentially proclaiming: "Fuck you all, work it out for yourselves, I am out of here!" as the last breaths leaked from spit-encrusted lips.

As a result of the various motivations surrounding the doctrines outlined in The Book, Erasure related murders commenced soon after. The Cult could in no way support such a thing; the purists suggested that these extreme measures were not part of the Natural Way, and that the Angels (a name given to the those in the interim phase of the afterlife) were part of The Way. Leaving the world without the subtle guidance of those gone before could only lead to chaos.

Still, the money flooded in to the Erasure team, who in the tradition of the rest of the organisation took on its own name – The Guild – named after significant discussion and storyboarding. For the most part the members of the team were mercenary by nature, and not really down with the quasi-religious rhetoric they had to endure from their clients. They were in it for the money, or the challenge. Few, if any, were in it for enlightenment.

The fees and the offers of fees that were paid to The Guild were staggeringly huge. A large portion of those fees went to The Cult. Like so many religious organisations before them, greed and the perceived need for more and more funds to do good works far outweighed the bitter taste of death.

# 20.

"If this is the case, why are you talking so freely about it? Aren't you afraid that you won't be able to pass while I remember you?" I asked the man across from me.

"I'm on the side of Angels," he said quietly, his old and worn face at odds with his fit and muscular body.

I had arrived at the meeting place, a little nervous at first to be meeting what might be one of the highest members of The Cult.

Then I chastised myself, thinking, "it's not actually a recognised religion. Why am I approaching this meeting with the same trepidation I would if talking to a Buddhist monk, or a nun, or some alleged miracle-working happy-clapper?"

In the months since I realigned my search methods I had focussed on anything that had had even the most tenuous link to the twin circle symbol. Poking and prodding at the forums I was careful not to repeat the mistake of just posting the image in the hope that someone would miraculously know everything about it and would gladly lead me by the hand to what I was searching for. Even though at times I was close to doing so, the sting of the previous fiasco had me too concerned to do it. My research was like a house of cards: carefully built, but at the whim of any draft that might gust through a hastily opened door.

I had ultimately become part of what is known as the Cult's crèche forum. Like a garden snail I entered, carefully passing the login threshold, I let my feelers gently probe their way about the forum, touch something, then retract and process the encounter. Touch something else. Process.

The culmination of all this work had led me to the table across from a man in a second floor apartment that had been converted to a kind of café cum artists' hangout above a leatherworks in Camden. It was the sort of place that if you had to ask its whereabouts, you'd never find it. Jealously guarded by the local folk, it was a haven away from the now heavy tourism surrounding London's famous market.

I followed the instructions given to me the week earlier, directing me to catch the tube to Camden Town station and then walk toward the market area. The leatherworks was next to a square that was home to five rows of t-shirt sellers, and I was to walk down the aisle closest to the leather works and stop at 'Java-t's' and ask the attendant: "Do you have anything different? I'm looking for a something less touristy?"

The bored attendant just looked at me and then got up. He waved at me, indicating I should follow, and moved to the back of the stall. He stood in front of a rack of particularly awful t-shirts and then looked over my shoulder, presumably annoyed by the sudden appearance of some more tourists. Their attendance in his stall was brief - the shoddy quality of the goods on offer along with the death-stare offered by my new companion was enough to have them waddle on their way, DSLR cameras hanging from brightly emblazoned neck-straps. Once the stall was clear, he moved the first arm's length of t-shirts aside, then said "Go."

I hesitated.

Obviously tired of waiting for this new dullard to work out what the score was he placed his hand in the small of my back and firmly pushed me into what appeared to be a rack of clothes.

Once beyond his arm length the t-shirts closed behind me, I took a couple of tentative steps toward a door in the wall that seemed to materialise in front of me, and knocked.

Like some back alley cliché, a sliding peep-hole opened and a pleasant voice asked me what I wanted and who had told me about the place.

"Coffee is what I want and the person who told me about the place should hopefully already be here – Martin? Is there a Martin here?"

The door opened swiftly and a hand reached out in greeting. The hand, once taken, greeted and pulled at the same time moving me quickly through the entryway, and into a stairwell.

The large door, old and well used, closed almost silently on its hinges, then the sound of a hasp being secured to lock it, along with the sound caused by the slight friction of the peep-hole being covered.

The doorwoman went back to sitting in a floral patterned high-back chair, and then reached to balance a cup of tea in one hand and a book in the other.

"Just go upstairs if you please," she said politely. "You'll see the door at the top of the stairs there," pointing now to a door visible through the balustrade of the stairs.

"Thank you," I said.

"You are very welcome," came the reply as she went back to her book.

*****

Martin was an amazingly easy person to talk to, and I asked him whether he would have found himself involved in a mainstream religious movement if he hadn't become involved in the Cult.

"I, like everyone else, had often given thought to the whole 'what next' argument. I dabbled in a few different belief structures but found them to be too restricting. People were being asked to be good to each other not because they had to, but because they feared some divine retribution would come spearing out of the sky."

He sipped his coffee.

"It's flawed," he continued. "Sure, it might work fine for the more pious amongst us, but for those who fall into the 'religious because I feel guilty' pile, all it does is build resentment. They would try to continue to be good people, but then see bad things happen to those that they loved and good things happen to those they despised."

I nodded. I could identify with that, although my argument had always been from a non-religious standpoint, and mostly uttered during drunken forum flare ups where I would fall back to the much asked question of why would a God allow horrible things to happen in the world.

Seeing that he had my attention, he went on: "The Cult made sense to me. I wished to be good and do good things, so that I might have an opportunity to help others in a very real sense once I die. That is where you get into heaven, not here. Not on earth."

"But you don't have to do good to be remembered, do you? You could be remembered for being a right evil bastard as well," I asked, and then chastised myself for swearing.

He didn't miss a beat and replied, "That's exactly the point though, your evil bastard might be wishing to be remembered so that he or she had the opportunity to have a longer intermediary life as an Angel, to achieve more good than bad over the two time spans."

I hoped it didn't show, but it was here that, for me at least, the bubble burst. While they were doing their best to be the complete opposite of religion, still, even in a Cult as young as this, they had already managed to incorporate an excuse to behave badly.

In fact, in the darker of minds it could almost be thought of as an encouragement: be more bastard-like and people will remember you, so you will have more time to do good in the intermediate life. There didn't seem to be any level of accountability in that plan.

I held it together as best I could. "But you choose to do good. Why?"

"Because it is in my nature to do good. I think the benefit of dabbling in the eastern religions enabled me to really take stock of what matters in life and what doesn't. Those teachings agree that most aggression stems from greed and jealousy. The trick though is to be above it." He paused to see if I was keeping up, and then pushed on.

"Even the good people that come here," he waved his hand around the half-full room as he spoke. "Even the most outwardly relaxed artist still covets the success of others. Not just to pay the bills, but usually to accumulate more... stuff. Even the most forward-thinking couple will come to a sickening crossroads if one strays away from the bed they share with their significant other. Where was I? Oh yes..."

Another sip of coffee and he continued.

"I regularly tell people that they should actively seek out the older eastern religions and take on board everything that they have to say about respect of others. I tell them to sift a little through the dogma to learn the lesson that happiness comes from within. When I do that one of three things happens." Martin put his cup down so he could count out on his fingers, "One: the person only wanted to be in an exclusive club so is discouraged that they can't just join and they go and find a less exclusive club to sneak into, like a biker gang. Two: they go away and study the ancient religions and, because they were teetering on the edge of becoming part of something anyway, they just stay with their preferred one. And three: they go to the other religions, learn what they need to learn, and then return to The Cult."

"So it doesn't bother you at all that people choose other paths, even after you've done your best to enlighten them?" I asked.

"No, not at all. We all end up in the same place. Some I'll end up travelling with, some I won't. It is not up to me to decide. Doesn't mean I don't take a passing interest in those that I meet though, which brings me to the question: which one of the three are you?"

"I'm definitely not of the first group. Of the other two, I like the way of older religions but am concerned that even they can be a tad hypocritical on subjects such as class and gender. So I guess I am teetering on option three," I replied, hoping that it didn't sound too much like a hastily put together answer at an important job interview.

Martin just smiled and said nothing more on the subject.

# 21.

I took up residence in Camden. I really liked that part of town, I even had brief delusions of returning here one day so I could just disappear into the crowd – only possible if I reached an end point in whatever game it was that I was playing.

The studio was at the Regent's Park end of Camden, a beautiful old park with a pleasant running track around it. I spent the first week doing nothing but running at dawn then home to breakfast and a brief check-in to the forums to make sure that all the irons I had placed in various fires weren't getting cold. Lastly I'd touch base with Bam. I'd then shower and head out to have morning coffee, making a show of approaching as many of the 'alternative lifestyle' shops and stalls I could find to ask about enlightenment classes, or yoga retreats or open nights where disciples of the various lifestyle groups would have poetry readings and discussions on 'the meaning of it all'.

I had messaged Martin to tell him about my intentions and new living arrangements; more to let him know that I was very much available and didn't have lengthy transport issues to contend with. He responded that he was always on the lookout for new coffee partners in Camden, and would keep in touch.

As we parted after the first meeting at the café, Martin had suggested that I could contact him any time I liked, but in practice this wasn't to be the case. It was two weeks before we met again, at the same café as before.

"We are having a gathering in a week, near to here. Would you like to come? It's a bit of an information night for those that are orbiting our group, and you'll have the opportunity to meet some likeminded people, some might even live here in Camden. How is the new place going?"

"Great," I said, and then without any need to lie, added, "I can't believe that I haven't been to Camden before, and now I live here! Well, at least I do for the short term."

We exchanged pleasantries and he asked about what I had been doing for the couple of weeks and was there anything I needed to know about the area. "The coffee is pretty good here at The Door, but it's not the best in town. For that you have to go to the bottom level of Camden Lock. There's a little roastery there, exceptional coffee."

"I'll keep that in mind," I'd actually had a cup from the place Martin was suggesting, but good manners suggested that I didn't mention it.

"You're a runner too," he said and I must have looked startled, because he went on, "Hah! No, I haven't been stalking you, I've just seen you occasionally while I'm out on my morning walk. You often run the outer circle road at The Regent's. I walk the inner paths. I would have said hello but you are far too fast for me."

We chatted amiably for about 45 minutes before he took his leave, I found myself warming to

Martin, and wondered briefly whether I was part of his plan to be remembered.

*****

The venue that was selected for the get together was a familiar one, a pub on the upper level of the Camden Lock. While I hadn't actually been inside the place I knew where it was as it was only a stone's throw from the coffee house Martin had recommended. I had taken his coffee recommendation as a gentle push toward being seen, as much as it was about the quality of the coffee, and as a result had become familiar with the area and businesses pretty well.

The pub in question looked like it had been refurbished recently: sleek black signs and intricate menus graced the doorway, the lettering on them could also be found on the black and gold disks adorning the beer taps along the bar.

The gathering took place at a most agreeable landing to the left of the bar where all of the tables had been removed and large cushions filled with rags were scattered, with firmer cube shaped ottomans serving as low drink stands.

I like to be on time, and am invariably the first one to any event, so I was pleasantly surprised to find half a dozen others already there and followed in a couple that I had been trailing since the train station.

One of the bar staff came to take our orders, and when I tried to hand over some money for my share of the large (and continually growing) order he smiled and told me that an amount of money had already been placed behind the bar and that should it run out, he'd let me know.

"Sorry," I replied, feeling the gaze of most of the others gathered up in our corner of the pub. "It's my first night here."

"You don't say?" he said, then turned back toward the bar. I smiled, there was no malice in his teasing.

"We've all done it. Shows the sign of a conscientious person, and the whole 'not being a burden' thing is endearing," said a voice beside me. It belonged to a guy who introduced himself as "Jay".

"Is that short for something?" I asked.

"Jay? It used to be. It's a long story. The upside is that it is easy to remember, particularly when drunk. That's got to be good a good thing, right?" he laughed.

"Indeed," I said and held out my hand to introduce myself.

"We're not as fresh to this whole thing as you, but not by much. Come and sit with us and we'll see how much of all of this we can work out together. It'll be like a pub quiz," he said, and put his hand on my shoulder in order to steer me to his little group.

The drinks arrived and so did Martin not long after. The small crowd, quite noisy until Martin's arrival, hushed. There was still talking and laughing, but at a more respectful volume. Martin looked around and noted my presence with a smile and a wave. Then strode over to where we were sitting and shook my hand, and gently rested his

Erasure.

free hand on my shoulder to prevent me the trouble of extricating myself from the cushion I was sharing with Jay. "No, no, don't get up, you'll only have to sit down again. I hope you are well," was all he said. After a protracted handshake, he smiled gently at Jay and the others in our little corner.

"Fuck. You know Martin?" asked Jay, with no small amount of awe. His friends Pat and Lisa had equally shocked looks on their face.

"I know him only well enough to have had coffee with him a couple of times, that's all," as the words tumbled from my lips I realised how smug I must have sounded.

"Wow," Jay said, still moving his gaze from me to Martin and back again. "You are going to be captain of this pub quiz, that's for sure". The last said as humour took the place of awe.

"If that's the case, Jay, you can kiss the grand prize of a bottle of house wine goodbye," I replied and took a large swig of my pint, hoping that someone would change the subject.

Thankfully, Lisa plunged into the conversation and discussed the origins of The Cult, and particularly its origins within the much older organisation, The Movement. It didn't take long for me to realise that with my hyper-connectedness and the luxury of a couple of months of trawling, I was the most knowledgeable on all things to do with the fundamentals of The Cult. I thought it prudent not to make mention of it though.

\*\*\*\*\*

Another round of drinks was produced and many guzzled the last of their previous drinks in a bid both to make space on the ottoman tables and keep up with the stream of free booze that was coming their way.

A short time later, Martin stood and introduced himself, the gathering stood in reply, and made a sign with their hands. Thumbs of both hands in contact with forefinger, the rest of the fingers at the same angle as the index finger. The hands were then brought together with fingernails laid flat against their corresponding partner on the opposite hand – like the shape that children make when they are trying to pretend their hands are binoculars – in this case though both hands were raised and tucked under the chin.

I looked at my hands and as I tried to make the sign and realised it was two circles, joined in at the centre.

Again I must have looked shocked, as Jay whispered: "It's okay, it's like a sign of respect. We do it at the gatherings, no big deal."

"Thanks Jay. No, I just look this way when I'm concentrating," I said and did my best to replicate those around me.

Martin looked over and singled me out as the newest member, "…and an early adopter of our unusual little ways, it seems," he said, as he in turn made the sign, then bowed slightly, smiling the whole time.

The gathering then just seemed to continue. I wasn't sure of what I was expecting but the lack of any kind of formal schedule had me confused. Was this just an extension of The Cult's crèche forum? Invite people to come to one spot, and watch them to see who is suitable?

Jay and pals were great company so I wasn't at all concerned about a wasted night. Although, I was becoming a little concerned with the amount of alcohol we were being plied with and on more than one occasion had to shake my head in the negative when the bar guy came over. This was met with howls and jeers, not just from my corner, but others within the room. The previous quiet and respectable group becoming a happy, if somewhat rowdy, mob.

Martin's attitude didn't change, or at least not outwardly. His smiling mask was fixed as he looked around the room, watching the groups as they interacted privately within their own little territories and more outwardly as groups started to interact with each other.

My refusal of drinks had begun to pay dividends, as many at the gathering had moved on from being socially-lubricated, to smashed-drunk.

Jay was nodding and staring at his pint in an effort to stay awake, his dreadlocked hair a wild tubular jungle that fell over his shoulders. Pat and Lisa were not quite as drunk, but had found their private discussion so stimulating that Pat had placed a smaller cushion over his lap and then set about fending Lisa's hand away from diving under it. Lisa pouted, then put her lips against his ear and said something that made his eyebrows shoot up. He turned to her and said, "Really?"

Lisa grabbed her phone and tapped a short message into it, which received a fast reply, the message indicator made just one loud ping. She held the phone up to Pat's face and he mouthed the return message. "Right, so when does she get home," he asked Lisa, a little breathless, but trying to keep his cool.

"She's there right now, all you have to do is say yes… you do want to say yes don't you?"

Pat gulped.

Lisa looked up and noticed I was watching the interaction: "Do you like women then?" she asked.

"Very much," I replied.

"Thought you would, it can be just so hard to tell sometimes, no offence."

"I guess it can be, and none taken," I said and laughed.

She turned her attention back to Pat and said, "Right then, we have a friend to visit." Pat flung his protective cushion into the corner and rose a little too quickly. He stumbled and then sat down, his legs folding neatly under him. Laughter followed due to Pat's look of complete confusion, and when Lisa managed to stop chuckling she got up, using the window sill as a prop and then offered her hand to Pat, who took it, stood, and managed to maintain his footing.

Jay had given up any pretext of trying to stay alert and had sagged into the cushion.

"What about Jay?" he asked.

"Ah yes, that age old question," said Lisa. "We'll walk him home, it's on the way after all."

"I can help him home," I offered. "I guess I'll be leaving shortly as well."

"Kind of you to offer, but when Jay is in that state he has a habit of not actually knowing where he lives. He usually just finds a bench to sit on until his memory returns, or the police pick him up. Never seems to bother him, says it's cheaper than a taxi."

I laughed.

"No," Lisa continued, "We'll take him, we know where he lives." She held out her hand in farewell and shook mine warmly. "Really hope we meet again, but I guess that's the point of these gatherings, isn't it? All so very underground," she said in a conspirital tone.

Pat half-waved and then shot out his hand as I offered mine, and after the three of us managed to raise Jay, they left, wobbling through the front door.

I had been having a good time, the first genuinely fun time I had had in a while. Through my slightly drunken haze came a voice chastising me for forgetting that some of these people might actually be only one step from Her killer. I sat back down to watch the crowd for a while, nursing my drink. I decided to wait for the next group to leave, and take that as my cue to sneak off in to the night.

I went to the bathroom and returned to find a full glass of wine placed next to my half-empty beer glass, and that Martin had moved to sit in my corner.

"It's a good corner this one, an excellent choice to see what is going on, I hope you've had a good time?" he said as I sat down.

"A great time. I've been sharing this corner with Jay and a couple of others. It's a really welcoming space you've got going on here," I said, the alcohol making my voice louder than I had intended.

Martin just smiled.

"Sorry, I'm a little drunk," I said.

"Not at all. You were drinking with Jay; a man whose intake has left far more resilient folk than you reeling about. You are doing just fine."

"That's good to know. He really can put it away, although if what you say is true I don't think he brought his A-game tonight," I giggled, thinking of Pat and Lisa who were probably at that moment assisting Jay into a cab.

"Indeed," said Martin, still with that fixed smile.

"Martin, I feel a bit like a free-loader, being here and not offering to help with the bill…"

"Think nothing of it, we own this building, part of the rent has always been that for our gatherings we have an open bar. It works well for all concerned."

"Handy, and in keeping tradition with the old Movement theme of meeting in public spaces," I said, and then worried if I had over-stepped the mark.

"Yes, the old myth of public forum," he lit a pipe, and no-one seemed to mind. "In the early years, we got as much done then in a meeting as we did tonight. People forgot after a while what it was they had come for in the first place. Too much emphasis on the game of arriving at the venue, not enough of what the group would actually do once there," he said wistfully.

"It was then that the factions began to sprout, and the reasons the Analysts were so protected and respected. They brought the information from all the factions together. Those meetings are much more private. Like the one you will be attending shortly," Martin was looking directly ahead, but his smile had diminished and was a little forced.

Something was wrong and all of a sudden I felt isolated. Not necessarily afraid, but I certainly wasn't happy where things might be going.

"With all respect," I began, "I am flattered at the invitation, but I think I might have to call it a night, perhaps I could come to the next one?" I hadn't moved to stand up. I was trying to remain calm.

"Oh, no, that wasn't an invitation. It was simply a statement. Your night is just beginning, I'd drink that wine while you can," he said looking directly at me this time. His mouth was still trying to maintain its trademark smile, but his face had changed. It might look like a smile at a distance, but close, it was a snarl. His breath, unpleasant, reaching out to me.

I rose and felt remarkably steady, picked up my satchel and made to move away.

"You won't get far and given the way some of our sentinels feel. You are probably safer if you stay right here with me," he said, patting my cushion.

Looking around, there seemed to be a few still enjoying the anonymous hospitality of the never-ending drinks tab, but amongst them were faces of those who looked very *very* sober all of a sudden, and any that glanced at me did so with such enmity that I realised it would be futile to leave until allowed to.

I sat down again.

"Very good decision," said Martin as he again lit his pipe.

# 22.

It was after midnight when the last of the freeloading attendees left, encouraged by those planted amongst the groups to say their goodbyes and leaving with parting words like: "If this is religion, sign me up." Or: "At least we adopted the whole wine thing from the Catholics."

Mostly they just showed up in front of Martin and told him how lovely he was, and thanked him for the hospitality. Drunker folk tried to act soberly, and much twin circle symbol-making was entered into, coupled with stiff bows. Martin magnanimously received the praise and wished them a safe journey home.

Once the last of the attendees were gone, the door was shut behind them. Martin turned to me, any vestige of humour drained from his face.

"Get up," he said, in a low voice.

I did, but more because it felt safer to stand rather than have my head at easy kicking level.

"Come with us," he said as he turned. Two of the remaining small group moved forward, no doubt to assist me to wherever it was we were going.

"I don't think I want any part of this," I said. "Not really feeling any connection to The Cult at the moment."

"You're connected already. The fact that we need to speak privately means that you are of interest. The figurative door you have been poking around only opens one way. You passed through it long ago. Now we need to know why you are here, and so we will speak in private."

I picked up my satchel and slung it over my shoulder, and noticed that Jay had left his crochet hat behind, and for whatever reason I picked that up too.

"Comfortable are you? Need help with your bags?" said one of my new escorts, with no humour at all in his voice.

"Comfortable? No, if you want to carry my bags you can go right ahead and add bag boy to what I am sure is a really impressive resume."

An open hand slammed into the side of my head, the heel of the palm striking just behind my ear, pushing me off balance and into the man I had just been trying to insult.

To his credit, he caught me from falling and said some harsh words to his escort partner, words I couldn't make out as my head was ringing from the force of the blow.

Martin had stopped to watch this little show and my predicament brought a smile back to his face. It was an ugly smile of joy, mirrored by a sadistic laugh that replaced the ringing in my ears as I slowly gained my bearings again.

Hands gripped each of my arms, an additional hand slipped in to the back of my jeans, lifting enough to make me feel that I would have to walk on tiptoe once we started moving. I was sobering, although still a little shaky. Even if I hadn't been, there was no way that I could have easily shaken the grip of my new friends.

The first of the two, the one who had stopped me from falling when I was hit by the other, leant toward me as we moved off in the direction of the door that Martin had disappeared through. "Sorry about Daniel," he said, I took it that he was talking about the guy who hit me. Something in the way he said it made believe that he was sincere.

*****

Through the door and down at least one flight of stairs, then out into the alley and into an adjoining building. In short order I was forced into a chair and strapped down. A bright light shone from somewhere a short distance away, and was trained on my face. The glare was blinding but I was aware of other people in the room, just not how many, nor where they were positioned.

A rearranging of chairs ensued, my captors were obviously getting themselves comfortable, and I had the feeling of more than a few pairs of eyes trained on me.

"Why are you here?" a voice, male, not Martin's.

"I'm here because you brought me here," I said.

Again, I was struck across the side of my head, the pain not as severe this time, but still leaving me momentarily dazed.

"How vulgar, Daniel, there is no need for that," a female voice.

Beside me, there was the sound of someone clearing their throat.

"Daniel, you and your little friend can sign off for the night. Run along outside, we have all the equipment we need. Run along now," came the new and patronising voice of an unknown man.

Movement in the periphery of my vision suggested that my escorts were immediately making ready to leave, one of whom (the nicer of the two) laid a hand gently on my shoulder as he departed.

"How touching, you're here for a couple of hours and you've made a friend already," said the female, then shouted, "Daniel, you need to talk to your little friend about his new job, and how he might need to start looking for a new one if he doesn't, what's the expression... harden the fuck up."

"Yes leader, I will talk to him immediately. Sure there is nothing else we can do?" asked Daniel.

"You've done quite enough, thank you. Shut the door, there's a good boy," she said.

"Now," the unknown male voice again. I still couldn't see but I was beginning to pick out positions by where the voice came from, and found this strangely comforting.

"Now, let's try that again, shall we? Why are you here? And try not to be funny, we are not particularly fond of jokes, particularly those told by strangers."

"I was invited by Martin," I said, figuring that if I kept the answers short I could stall the amount of information that they would be able to take. I was unsure of what I was stalling for, but it was the closest thing I had to a plan.

"Someone needs to apply the power source. Daniel should have done it before he left, instead of being so violent. Martin? Can you do the honours?" the female said.

A shadow walked through the light briefly allowing me to confirm that there were three others besides myself and Martin in the room. There was the female, who seemed to be in charge of whatever this part of the adventure was becoming; the condescending male who spoke as I was being seated; and another to the right of where I sat, who hadn't uttered a word.

Martin had circled around the chair, then came back with something heavy and placed it in my lap. It was a car battery and wires were retrieved from the arms of my seat, newly attached spring clips gripped and bit in to the soft lead of the battery terminals.

A warm feeling coursed from my tailbone to the top of my spine, a slight ringing in my ears washed in to my thoughts. Different from the sound that had erupted from the blows administered by Daniel.

"What are you doing?" I said, growing fearful or the first time in a long while. "What the fuck have I done to deserve this? I wanted to find out about The Cult, I was invited here, I came, and now you are about to torture me? What kind of religion is this?"

Pain shot up my spine and threatened to make me lose control of my bodily functions. It only lasted a second, but it was enough to make me scream. I could feel the warmth of the electrode, nothing more than a ridge that ran from the front of the seat to the back, rising steeply to make as much contact with the soft areas around and under my genitals.

I had noticed it when I sat down but had given it no consideration; I didn't expect an interrogation seat to be comfortable so I figured it was part of the way the seat was formed, like some Swedish design ploy. Now I knew what the ridge was for, I tried to move away from it but the way the chair was built was ingenious, and every movement only seemed to seat me more effectively on the electrode.

Robert Smith's voice entered my head singing part of The Cure's song 'Lullaby': "Don't struggle like that or I will only love you more…."

Even through jeans it was excruciating, but thankfully the pain receded as quickly as it had arrived.

"Painful isn't it, my little fly. It will only become more interesting as time wears on, particularly if we have to throw water on you to make sure that nasty little connection is working at its full potential."

"I don't understand what the hell it is you want from me," I said, sweat beading on my brow. "Why this? Why not just ask me?"

"Because you are very good at covering your tracks is why, this will make sure at least some of what you tell us is true," the woman said. "Now, if you please, answer my fucking question." The last said with such venom I was, for a moment, lost for words.

"Why are you here?" the question came again, from the man this time.

I paused to gather my thoughts, but apparently this only served to infuriate whoever held the controls to the chair, so another second-long period of warm pain rushed through me.

"This will not stop until we get answers, we have many car batteries, and the night is still very young."

"Why are you here?" the woman again.

"I am looking for information on The Cult. Martin met me, and then he invited me here tonight."

"That is closer to the truth, but still close to your original answer. I'll let that pass for now."

I breathed out with a sigh.

"Let me clarify my request a little more: Why would you leave your country, travel all the way here, just to live in a bed-sit in Camden? The cost of which would surely be surpass whatever free beer you could consume…"

"I came into a significant amount of money and I wanted to feel more connected to this life, so I started searching for religious groups that are not part of the mainstream," I said, hoping that the well-practiced statement didn't sound too wooden.

"Quite laudable intentions. Tell me though, where did this cash you acquired come from?"

"An insurance policy my partner had taken out. She died, I got the money, and a reason to search deeper into what life was all about." Not entirely untrue, but the fear of the chair and the vulnerable position I found myself in had me worried about how long I could stretch this out. Each answer followed by a second or two of horrific and terrible waiting. Would there be a jolt? Or not? Fear and expectation had me concerned that I might piss myself; another full-power jolt and the remaining control over my bladder might be completely removed.

"Died did she?" the male voice said. "Did that of her own free will, did she? Get tired of hanging around, did she?"

I reeled. 'Hanging around'? Was that an obtuse remark about the hammock in the yard at the beach? Had I landed square in the midst of people who had something to do with Her?

Another pulse ran through the chair, less powerful this time, whether that was due to the battery or not I don't know, and I obviously didn't tell them of their contraption's short fallings - I was hardly going to help them be more effective.

What I guess to be the adrenaline let loose by fear and near panic made my heart race, but seemed also to slow time, and heighten my senses. The bright light, combined with sweat running into my eyes, had reduced my vision, but I could hear people on the cobble outside – probably late-night alley stalkers looking for booze or other pastimes. Over the musty odour of the room was a familiar and weirdly comforting smell. Coffee. I could smell coffee. Was I near the coffee house?

Had Martin been giving me a clue as to where I would ultimately end up? Or maybe he had been passively encouraging me to go somewhere that I could be more easily watched so that my reasons for being in Camden could be pieced together from day to day conversations.

Another pulse, much stronger. I was in danger of pissing myself and the knowledge of that made me angry. Pain I could cope with, at least for now. The humiliation of being at the whim of these crazy people along with pissing on their floor was more than I wanted to deal with.

"Fuck! What?" I shouted, "I answered your question."

"No you didn't. How did she die?"

"What does it matter? She's dead, and I am alone in a room with you people, how she died is none of your business." I waited for another blast through the chair, but it didn't come.

"Everything is our business, or we make it our business. Either way, you are still avoiding being frank and honest with us."

"Hard to do when I'm tied to a chair in some fucked up B-movie torture cliché," I said.

Laughter filled the room. Even the man who had not made a sound until this point was genuinely laughing.

"Oh you are a funny one," he said, once he had gained control of his mirth. "For ages it seems I have been saying that this form of trying to extract information from people is a little...passé." He then addressed the others in the room, "I told you, but you wouldn't listen. The dark room, the bright light, car battery. Electrocution techniques are so ineffective, and you labelled that poor grunt Daniel for being barbaric."

"No," he said, returning his attention to me, "we need to be more innovative, and it has taken someone from across the sea to come all the way here to educate us poor feeble folk on how we should do things. You are that someone, you are the messiah if you will. Here to help educate us in the ways of torture so exquisite. I am looking forward to the lesson. Unfortunately, it will have to be trial and error of course, and we'll have to use just the tools we have at hand. I'm sure though that your message will be conveyed, in time."

A chill ran through my body. I heard movement as he stepped toward me, a hand, his hand, mashed heavily across my face, covering it, the smell of bar snacks evident, as was the roughness of his palms.

Two noises followed as first one and then the other clamp were removed from the battery. Then the sound of the caps being pulled from the battery's reservoirs and, finally, the weight of the thing was removed from my lap.

He stood as a silhouette in the light, the battery held out so as not to touch him, then moved behind me as I struggled to see what he was doing.

A grunt and a wet trickling noise could be heard, like a toppled container laying on its side and emptying.

The noise stopped and fluid was running through my hair. "I'd keep your eyes shut if I were you. The battery water might sting a little." He was emptying the contents of the battery over my head.

"It probably feels quite refreshing right now, but battery acid is a funny thing. It waits, just a little

156

while, before it makes it presence truly known. Then it creeps into your skin, a little itchy at first, then it will start to burn. Etching into your soft skin, burning and bleaching. If you are good, we'll wash you down. If not, as I mentioned before, we have no shortage of batteries, and you have much more sensitive skin to apply their contents to."

"We'll be back soon," he said while walking back past the light. "I'm sure you would like to be alone with your thoughts for a while. The last twenty minutes has been such thirsty work. Feel free to scream when the burning starts, we'll take that as a cue to return for the information we require."

Rustling noises and a closing door. The room was empty, but for me, and the faint smell of coffee.

# 23.

The bindings on my arms were Velcro and far more efficient than I would have expected for a fastener of cheap shoes and stripper pants. One loop of it covering my forearm along its length. Another much broader loop that had some elasticity was wrapped around my mid-section – but my legs were free, which I found unusual. While I wasn't in the habit of getting fastened to a chair, I reasoned that leaving a captive's legs free must make people who come within kicking distance quite vulnerable to attack.

My appraisal of the bindings holding me to the chair wasn't completely thought through. My critique quickly fell apart during a concerted struggle to break free when it became apparent that the chair was bolted to the ground and, as I was firmly attached to the chair, the only thing in danger would be someone's shins should they be standing too close and directly in front of me.

These musings were obviously some kind of post-adrenaline pre-shock condition, if nothing else they kept me focussed on the mechanics of how I was attached. Until the itching started, and then the gentle burning that followed. It wasn't as excruciating as I thought it would be, but it had potential. "I need to get out of here quickly," I thought.

Muffled noise and what I later guessed correctly to be shouting came from the room my captors had disappeared into. Then, what sounded like a gunshot rushed under the door.

Someone was out there, and they weren't happy. All I could hope was that they knew I was here.

Soon after the shot, the old lock rattled in the door and, as it swung open, a new light source leaking through the door caught my attention. The bulb shining in my face was shut off, and there were now six people in the small dank room.

The laughing guy who was no longer laughing, The two pompous questioners, Martin clutching at his arm, me…and Jay.

"Someone needs to do some untying. Martin, you look least likely to cause a fuss now, what with that new little scratch on your arm, why don't you do it?"

Martin didn't move.

Jay pointed the gun toward Martin's head and said: "Or don't, I don't care. No one here will report you dead, for fear of all the file-changing that they'd have to commission."

Martin breathed heavily and took a step forward then stopped, before continuing toward me. He used his damaged arm to pull at the bindings. Blood oozed through the fingers of his good hand as it applied pressure to the new wound in his arm. I was quickly freed. Rising fast, I stood and immediately raked my hands through my hair.

I pulled off my t-shirt, and grabbed my bag and jacket where they had been thrown zipping the jacket up to my chin and slinging the bag over my shoulder.

"Come on Jay, let's go."

Jay hesitated, then waved me toward the door, as Laughing Guy spoke, "They obviously don't make batteries like they used to. Perhaps we should have stuck to the old rules of engagement – torture and rape you until you are broken, then ask questions. Sometimes innovation can be a double edged sword."

Jay responded by slamming the butt of his pistol into Laughing Guy's temple. It didn't knock him out, but Laughing Guy dropped to his knees, and then looked up at me.

"All of this won't make any difference to what happened to your hammock-loving friend… "

Jay hit him again, and Laughing Guy fell heavily to the ground, unconscious. It spoke volumes about the intestinal fortitude of the others in the room that none of them moved to help their companion as they backed away as soon as Jay turned his attention to them.

Jay waved at the door again, but instead of leaving, I went to the limp wreck that was Laughing Guy and went through his pockets retrieving a wallet and a phone. I then demanded the same of the other three.

"Hard up for cash are you?" asked Jay.

"No, just an insurance policy to give us a bit of a head start," I replied.

I took great delight in having their personal things placed in my hand, but couldn't resist frisking them anyway. The woman in particular was reviled at my attentions; a reaction that made the exercise even more worthwhile.

After getting what I needed, I left through the door and waited for Jay. As my eyes adjusted, it turned out to be as I had expected: a back room of the coffee house. I went through the wallets and the woman's handbag and retrieved all the cash I could, which turned out to be quite a lot. Then turned all of the mobile phones off and stuffed them in my satchel.

Jay followed and closed the door behind him.

"I've already organised for a bin to be placed in front of the door in the alleyway and the coffee boys will have to miss out on business tomorrow morning because I'm going to foul the front door lock, along with this one," pulling a tube of glue from his pocket, he injected the lock with adhesive.

"The coffee boys, are they in on this?" I asked.

"In on what? This capture and question thing? No, The Cult just owns this building, and gives them cheap rent provided they keep that back room free."

"Martin told me to come here…"

"It is the best coffee around, maybe he was just dealing with his guilt. Weren't you Martin?" He called out in case they were listening on the other side of the door.

A muffled expletive came in reply.

I left one hundred pounds on the cash register, explaining to Jay the it might help compensate the coffee-guys for the lost business.

Jay smiled and said, "I knew you were one of the good ones."

We left, and as soon as Jay sabotaged the door, we ran – Jay grabbing a small duffle bag from a nearby doorway as we passed.

*****

We headed in the direction of Regent's park, running in the dark places, walking in where streetlights lit the shadows. There was a large amount of cash left at my flat, along with the two money cards so I told Jay that we'd have to sneak by. "We're going to need money," I said.

"Yes, I thought I had better watch you. Didn't think I'd actually need to perform a rescue so I'm a little under-prepared myself."

My street was deserted, but still we were both on edge.

Jay took the lead, "It's going to be watched. I'll go. Until our tortuous little friends get out I can still be a nobody. Just."

I gave him my key, then hid behind a low wall in someone's front garden and watched him stumble away, a reprise of the act he put on at the gathering.

He was good. He looked catastrophically drunk and even stopped apparently to vomit in the neighbour's pot plant. Then he was inside.

He had asked where everything was inside the apartment and was glad that the instructions were simple. It was a tiny place anyway, and as I had always been ready to up and leave, it was just a matter of him getting in to retrieve the cash and cards from their hiding place and then get out.

After twenty minutes I became concerned, he was away much longer than I had expected. Had he been met on the stairs? Thankfully, there was no gunfire to be heard and none of the other apartments had turned their lights on, so there couldn't have been a scuffle.

A man was walking toward my hiding place from the opposite direction and I froze. He had a shaved head and wore a t-shirt and thigh length jacket. Sitting on the low wall, he lit a cigarette. He put one of the bags he was carrying on the wall where it fell, landing right next to where I crouched. Swearing, he turned to retrieve it and looked directly at me.

It was Jay.

He let out a low "shhhhhhhh" as he grabbed up the bag. Then pulled out a phone and dialled someone.

"Yeah, Marcus? You awake? You're not going to make me fookin' walk are ye?" he said, completely different to the accent from before. "Fook you ye coont, I'm fookin' freezen', me. Okay? Okay."

He turned toward me and put his cigarette out on the top of the wall. Speaking low and from the corner of his mouth he said, "Car coming, be ready."

It was probably only ten minutes before the car rolled slowly to a stop in front of Jay, but it felt like hours. Twice he had to fend off enquiries for cigarettes and dope, which he managed to do by continuing with the gruff persona he had cultivated since going into my apartment.

"Now," he said as the driver got out of the car and the two men embraced and swapped a loud joke, a smoke screen for me to dive into the back seat. Once I was safely in, the guys, without apparent need to hurry, made their way into the car as well.

"Stay down for fuck sake," said the driver, smiling at something that Jay had apparently just said.

The thud of a closed fist crashed on the trunk of the car. Someone else was there. The ruse was over, and we sped off into the night.

# 24.

The drive to the safe house took thirty five minutes. The first part of which was taken up by Jay talking to the driver (who introduced himself only as Milke) about some of the night's events. There didn't seem to be a pattern to what he told Milke, but figuring that he must have a reason I didn't try to correct him. The last part of the journey Jay and the Milke discussed what would be best to do about my hair and more particularly my scalp, which was itching unbearably.

"Just cut it all off," said Milke, "It will solve a whole mess of potential problems."

"What do you think about that?" Jay asked me.

"I'm hardly a fashion plate to begin with," I said, at that moment sitting on my hands to distract them from raking at my scalp. "The rest of me is fine, my hair just must have retained the water or whatever you call the stuff that comes out of a battery."

"Couldn't have been that strong if it's only itching," said Milke.

"A small mercy," I replied.

On entering the safe house, I launched myself at the bathroom and proceeded to strip off and shower. I doubted if removing my hair was necessary but decided to cut it off anyway. It felt right, almost a cathartic thing, a feeling that overshadowed both my medical concerns, and any deep-seated thoughts I might have had relating to vanity.

Soon after, I crawled into the bed that Jay had allocated for my use. Exhausted, I sank into the realm of dreams as quickly as a pebble disappears into a pond.

*****

The following morning I set about attempting to connect my laptop to whatever was left of my network. I wasn't expecting much, as the events of the night before were likely to have had a pretty negative effect on the forums I was involved with. In particular those close to the heart of The Cult. The frustration of not knowing, along with the apparent inability of my phone to reliably connect to my laptop was making my eye twitch.

"What are you doing?" Jay asked while stifling a yawn. An action that intimated that, even though he was interested, his laid-back manner was about as overtly concerned as he was going to get.

"Calm down," I said, grinning at him. "The machine is tunnelled and the phone routed so many different ways that while it still lists as a phone call or data connection from here, it won't actually know it is me. Every day a new number and name get appended to this sim card. It's a complete blank with respect to tracking."

Jay smiled, and got up from the low futon couch he had been lazing on and pulled up a chair beside me. I had commandeered the small dining table for the purposes of carrying out something that felt like a plan. Or at least the making of one. Perhaps it was the remnants of the adrenaline-dump my system had had to deal with the night before, but I felt that I had to be doing something.

The phone's tethering link dropped again.

"I know this might sound a little, you know, regressive, but have you considered going old school and maybe just use a cord to plug your phone into your laptop?" Jay asked.

I looked at him and feigned a grimace.

"I know, a little out there in the thinking department," he said waving his hands around as if ideas were bees and they were circling his head.

"My point is this..." I began. He placed his head in his hands and stared at the phone, then the computer, then me.

"Oooh, a story, go on then," he smiled again.

"Stop it. Now, my point. What use is having a wireless connection, a technology that must have cost millions of dollars to develop, only to have it not work, or at the very least, not work consistently?"

"You don't want me to actually answer that do you?" he stated, then continued, "this is some kind of miniature protest you are waging, right?"

"Someone has to."

"Hard to stage a protest when you are operating through a tunnelled laptop," he said, and smirked.

"Still not the point I...Wow!" I uttered as the screen again went black and my reflection came in to focus on the shiny screen.

"Wow what?" asked Jay.

"It's just going to take a while before I get used to having no hair," I replied.

"Could be worse, you didn't know it before you got the invitation, but the people in that private party you found yourself in are bad bastards. Bad. Bastards," he said.

"Yes, they didn't seem so friendly. No canapés on arrival or anything. The thing that surprised me most was how different Martin was to the way he portrays himself to the world. That silver tongue of his must recruit hundreds of people to the cause," I said.

"You're right, he does a lot of the gathering. Primarily because he is head of 'marketing', for want of a better term. Really, he heads a team that chases threads and draws people into The Cult. Most of The Cult and Movement sites on the web, both in the Google-style front side and in the forum wastelands, are probably managed by his team. Or at least significantly influenced by them."

Once he had finished sharing this little piece of information he glanced at my computer, then got up and moved back toward the couch.

"That's it?" I asked.

"No, but your link still isn't working, it's probably a driver," he said and picked up his satchel from the sofa, opened it, and then started flailing about in its contents.

"Fuck it," I said, staring at both the laptop and the phone in the misguided belief that I could make them link out of abject fear of my wrath. They both just blinked, mocking me.

Jay returned from rummaging around in his bag and tossed me a cord.

"What's that?" I asked.

"A cord? A connection? Most of all it's an enabler. It will enable you to connect your technologies, with the added bonus of enabling me to stop being so mean-spirited toward you and your stubbornness."

I plugged the cord into both the phone and laptop and was only a little perturbed that it worked immediately.

"Just so I know you aren't about to bring a swarm of Cult monkeys down upon us, I'd like to take a look at this tunnel of yours, if I could." He slid the laptop around so he could get at the keyboard, opened a command window and entered a few more strings of code and hit enter.

A stream of data sped up the screen.

"Shit, this is some kind of tunnel. This is art in pure binary form. Not many people can come up with this kind of stuff, the only one I know with this kind of talent disappeared a few years ago. The others are dead or so deep into The Cult they'd never allow this sort of gear out of their sight, let alone load it onto a laptop. There's no signature code in it though. Usually authors add a code to stamp their presence out of sheer vanity," Jay said, genuinely awestruck by what he was seeing.

"I've spent a lot of time with the person that loaded this, she's really not one for putting her name about the place. Apart from the time I've been here in England, I have all but lived with her for the previous year or so, and I still only know her by her online name."

"What name?" said Jay, serious and attentive.

"Bammer, is the name I know her as," I said.

Jay sat bolt upright, and looked at me like I had summoned someone from the dead.

"No wonder Martin and his cronies are interested in you. Her real name is Belinda Hammond" he said.

*****

I had no idea what it meant. I had suspected that Bammer knew something but had been holding back. Over time I had reasoned that she was she was a defector of sorts, and most of the information she had stored away in that imperfect brain of hers wasn't likely to make sense if spoken aloud. I'd simply rationalised that her talents and knowledge were best applied in the mechanics of what we had been doing while sifting around in the murky data wasteland.

I *was* reasonably sure that she wouldn't let me just saunter into the lion's den if I didn't have to, but then she was an unusual unit, her reality somehow different to anyone else I had ever met.

It seemed strange that she was known by people high enough in a secret organisation to be all but anonymous themselves, and yet not once in six months had she mentioned, apart from telling me about her early involvement, that she used to be a valuable cog in this large and ungainly machine.

She knew everything I was searching for, and why I was searching. Yet, besides giving me a conduit to utilise, she gave me no guidance whatsoever in who to talk to or what portal or forum

I should have been considering to get through to the people who murdered Her.

Jay was still staring at the computer:

"This tunnel is so effective at masking your location that the absence, the sheer void of any tell-tale tracker suggests that this is the work of someone really good. Someone who used to be involved in The Movement or The Cult. The coding is weapons-grade stuff, but now that I know who made it, it is the quality of this work that smacks entirely of Bel… Bammer. It's why she didn't sign the code internally, it couldn't have been created be anyone else."

"What does it MEAN though Jay? If you know just tell me, because it's doing my head in."

I got up and strode to the kitchen – both to collect my thoughts and slake my sudden thirst for a cup of coffee. As soon as the kettle could be heard Jay placed his order, "If you're making one, I'll have white with no sugar thanks."

I opened every cupboard in the kitchen only to find that the all of the crockery was in a pile on the sink - teetering as the grey morning light shone through the window. I selected the two least cracked cups and washed them as best I could, then started looking for coffee.

"On the bench, next to the toaster," Jay called, and added, "this code is a thing of beauty."

"You sound like you are getting a little misty-eyed there. Careful, no tears on the keyboard." I said, then pulled the lid from a timber canister and found the sugar I was looking for.

"How is she? Bammer?" asked Jay when I had returned with two cups of cheap awful coffee.

"She is…"

"Still carving holes in her legs is she?" he said, stone faced.

"Not much space left to carve, I am afraid. She has moved to her arms, I think it is only sheer brute force of will that stops her taking a knife to her face."

"She was part of one of the early experiments, one in which The Cult had theorised that if files could be changed it might alter the way people were remembered, but if a person could be impregnated with the idea that they needed to change the way they looked, then it would confuse the memories of those around them. Their loved ones would have multiple versions of the individual to process. A kind of self-erasure if you will."

"I don't understand. If someone felt so strongly about being forgotten and that someone wanted it bad enough, why would they need to be brainwashed to do so? It seems a bit redundant given the lengths that people will go to be forgotten," I said.

"It's a weird concept, but consider that this technology wasn't to aid those who actively want to be forgotten – they had got on the plastic surgery train already. The concept was to aid their loved ones who mightn't share the same beliefs to achieve the short transition goal without knowing they were doing it. Those supporting the scheme, in their misguided wisdom, felt they had some altruistic opportunity to help those around them." He took another sip of his coffee, "Essentially messing up consistent memory of their loved ones by changing the very thing that makes people recognisable – their physical features…"

My mind scratched about trying to grasp what Jay was saying. Although comprehension was close, it was dancing just outside the light of the conversation.

"…and you need to understand that, at the time, this hypothesis was considered cutting edge, if you'll pardon the awful pun. People became desperate in their beliefs, almost evangelical. In short, they thought it was their duty to do such things for those they loved."

Jay paused again to see if any of the information was sinking in. It was, and I felt sick.

"Bam was part of the project," said Jay, pushing on. "She created the data matrix that would blast the brain into thinking this way. Unfortunately no-one could foresee what the strength of such a radical change would do. The hope was that people would be compelled to seek out plastic surgery. It was never meant to make them hate themselves. Just working with the data so closely caused this psychological rift in her. They called it 'The Sickness'. She was the only survivor of the experiment, and she wasn't even a subject."

"Shit."

"Yes," said Jay. "Shit indeed."

"How did it work?" I asked, even though I was not sure I'd be comfortable with what he said next.

"The Sickness? Ingenious really. A virus was placed into the subject's life file..."

"Life file?"

"The file that contains a person's complete set of connections and potential connections, all their comings and goings, purchases, interests..." Jay said, not knowing that Bammer had shown me my very own file.

Jay continued: "Once the virus is placed and activated, the subject is bombarded with media relating to body image and social opinion targeted to sound like the opinions are aimed directly at the person involved. That media can be deployed easily by way of Internet advertising that pops up on search engines. It can arrive in the form of additional 'sponsor' information that can simply be added to anything posted from a mailing list. Public transport ad space can be accessed and purchased simply by checking the route a person takes to work and transport they take. SMS messaging directed at their phones. Digital television is easy to patch into, so stories and advertising can be shovelled at the subject that way too. The scope and frequency is staggering," Jay paused, and then shook his head "On paper it looked like a great idea, in practice it was devastating."

My head swam, not only because Bammer had created and then inadvertently been subject to The Sickness, but Jay spoke with such authority I began to wonder how deep he had been in the whole mess.

I had warmed to Jay, it was hard not to, but I found his revealing insights into The Cult disquieting. I was also aware that he had the ability to withhold information, easily. I understood that the driver that picked us up in Camden might not have needed to know the complete minute by minute rundown, but the things he excluded were calculated.

That he seemed to know Bammer really well was a shock. Of course if he had told me that he knew her while he had adopted his drunken hippy persona when we first met it would have been almost inconceivable. Now though, particularly after all his efforts that potentially saved my life, it wasn't that far a stretch.

Bam used to work deep in the hornet's nest I was poking at. Jay had some kind of para-military thing going on, and was actively fishing next to a dangerous pond, wrestling whatever was in it with his bare hands. Given the more than unusual situation I had found myself in, I shouldn't have been surprised that there could be some kind of connection.

"How do you know Bammer?" I asked, trying to keep the accusatory tone from my voice. The room felt colder; I had let down my guard and felt the need to reappraise this new relationship.

"It's a long story, but we'll have time to go over that. What is more important now is that we stay out of sight and certainly keep our faces out of any cameras."

"Given my position I'm not entirely comfortable with you knowing so much about me, and me not knowing anything about what your connection to

Bammer is… and what that connection means." I said.

"Look, given your position, you are just going to have to trust me," he replied.

My concern only continued to deepen.

"I am not avoiding the issue," he was standing now. "It's just that now is not the time. It's going to take a while to try to shake the hounds off our scent so we'll have plenty of time to discuss my relationship with Belinda, I promise. You are more than welcome to go it alone if you wish, but as you saw last night, you are in very grave danger."

I nodded. He was right. If I was looking for motives to at least stick with Jay for a while longer, his arrival to drag me out of a place where I'd been plied with electric shock and battery acid was a pretty compelling one.

Resuming his happy-go-lucky persona he said, "I'm going for a shower. One that I would have had last night but someone else managed to use all the hot water. Something about battery acid and chairs and dark rooms and 'Oooo my head is itchy'" he hopped from foot to foot and rubbed at his head as if his hair (if he had any) was on fire.

In spite of the misgivings that were bouncing around in my head, I laughed, and so did he.

"Listen, we both agree it's a shit situation, but I'm on your side. We haven't got around to discussing why you're here at all. Let's just see how this goes, hey?" he held out his hand and we shook, sealing at temporary truce.

# 25.

For two weeks we moved from safe house to safe house, travelling as far and as wide as we could travel, all the time staying within the UK to avoid, at least for the time being, the formalities of border control. Sometimes we would travel for four hours only to stay long enough to sleep for a few more, then travel back to where we started.

We took public transport, we hired cars, we cycled; but no matter what our mode of transport, we made certain that we didn't follow any pattern, other than to move. Always move.

While either travelling or waiting I pieced Jay's story together from several conversations. He kept on referring to 'the work' or 'his work', whenever he talked about his involvement in The Cult.

He covered again what Martin had said in the coffee house in Camden, about Factions and how they were the downfall of The Movement. He went on to say that The Cult had originally been formed in the spirit of saving the good parts and discarding the bad. The intent was to add the spiritual focus that had often been discussed in the groups, and make it a core component

Jay explained that before long the factionalism they were trying to dispose of bubbled to the surface and when it did, the differences weren't just about group-management.

The more relaxed of The Cult, the 'Angels', went about the business of being remembered in order to prolong the middle-ground before having to stride off into the afterlife.

The more conservative faction -The Monastics - believed that by understanding the ramifications and manipulating their existence, they could reduce their memory footprint, and so shorten the time they had to stay in limbo. As a result, they tended to live secluded lives where possible, with the wealthier of those who chose the Monastic lifestyle actively engaged in behaviour to make sure the memory of them was limited.

It was extraordinarily hard to succeed as a Monastic; all it took was a newspaper report or scandal to have them shoved back into the spotlight, and therefore back into the mainstream of public memory. For the most part, failed Monastics took a moderate approach when returning to the The Cult proper. Many simply gave up on The Cult altogether if they were outed.

Some, though, were so ashamed about losing their elite positions in the secretive ranks of the Monastics that they turned full circle and embraced The Angel way of life.

This wasn't without its troubles.

Some of those returning to the mainstream of The Cult had, during their time as a Monastic, chosen the darkest of paths - those of murder and deep corruption of files in order to ensure their own disappearance from public and private record. They didn't take too kindly to being brought out of their hermitage, and often resolved to continue their methods but wanted to achieve an opposite outcome to that they had previously sought.

This last group, the so called 'Black Angels' jumped into the opposite side of The Cult with gusto, choosing to be remembered for their horrific acts and their inhumanity, thus ensuring a long intermediate life in which they could influence those left on earth. The system they employed had been nurtured while locked away as a Monastic, and was easily transferred to this new purpose. Moreover, it was deemed that it was simply part of their makeup.

Jay had considered himself a moderate Cultist, with a preference for The Monastic side, but more as a concept than an extreme life choice.

His talents brought him to the attention of The Cult. He and a few others found themselves in the middle ground. They formed the working rank and file; the paid machine that kept all the factions on course.

Because of the way the work impacted those in many factions, workers were secretive, rarely openly declaring their exact theological position within The Cult. The reason for this was to keep parties with conflicting interests in the dark about the various operations that people such as Jay undertook. In most cases, workers were employed by someone on one side of The Cult in carrying out actions that affected the machinations of the other. These actions became the ebb and flow of the fledgling religion.

The safe house system that Jay and I were using was created as a network for workers to be able to have safe spaces wherever they went. These safe houses were particularly useful once the end game of a job had come to pass and the worker needed to disappear, quickly.

The work varied, but it was always well paid, although Jay's tasks were more limited in scope. He did much of his work for the Monastics – silently moving about the cities and suburbs of the world, forever changing his ways in order to blend in as much as he could.

His primary job was the removal of hard copies of photos and files. Many times he did this by befriending the very people he was to steal from. Staying in character for months at a time to remove a single item or a whole filing cabinet from their house. His benefactors had money and time; all that mattered was that he got the job done.

"There was other work that I carried out. I'm ashamed of it. So very ashamed." he said once, ending that night's conversation.

Bammer also became a worker. She had always been smart, acing her way through her data-management degree, only to find herself back at the same university offering lectures on Deep-Data Tracking and offering her findings on many of the projects she had begun.

Lecturing was hell for her though, as her almost crippling shyness caused severe anxiety attacks before and after the classes, so she offered most of her lectures drunk, or stoned.

The attendees didn't care. What she was talking about, indeed, what she had already achieved in her research, was visionary.

However, the need to prop herself up in order to disseminate the information was resulting in behaviour that threatened to affect the thing she cared about most: Deep-data. For her it was simply beautiful – a symphony welling out of the machine, her fingers assisting a thousand instruments to be heard in the music.

In time, she quit lecturing and opened a consultancy, hoping that by consulting she would be able to work alone in the comfort of her own space. An arrangement that made her very happy and, in equal measure, successful.

Almost from the outset she was inundated with work from the commercial sector, mostly market optimisation and product logistics. Then work started coming in from private individuals imploring her to utilise her talents and the programs she had designed to find things, files, and people.

So, she did, and embraced this new and previously unconsidered income stream. It was direct, it was hard, but it seemed to hold some kind of integrity. Even in the short time she had been helping large corporations she realised that, the larger the company, the less likely they could be trusted with the information she supplied. So she cut them off and focussed wholly on the smaller and, strangely, more lucrative clients.

Her corporate clients tried to get her back on side by offering more and more money. She declined.

Deep-data processing was her baby, her child; not something to be sent out to glittering offices in large glass plated buildings to be whored and abused.

The work she could do for individuals was far more nourishing. In time, it worked out that the individuals she worked for were at times very much like herself: many were interested in data and it's ability to connect people. After a while, and via a couple of pertinent emails to and from clients, she found out about The Cult, and embraced it. Her work became even more dynamic and diverse. For the first time in her working career she felt comfortable working in a team, and her ability to work remotely calmed a lot of her anxieties.

Bammer was in geek-nirvana. Her entire job was based on the thing that she loved the most and did best. As a result, she was left to scour and scrape data for every possible instance of whatever it was that she was commissioned to find. The team would then act upon the information. Everyone got paid and then got up to do it again the following day.

It took a while for the team to actually meet face to face. It turned out that it was a pretty small group – just Bammer, and Jay.

All factions of The Cult wanted something done, but The Angels wanted more public presence, not of The Cult as a whole, rather the individuals within The Cult.

Since it was never part of The Cult's charter to step into the lime-light, The Cult never really got behind a marketing push for new membership. If there was one thing all members agreed upon, it was that people should search out want they wanted, not simply be dragged toward Cult membership by a good marketing slogan. It was one of the lingering principles left over from days of The Movement.

The work that came from anyone involved in The Monastics was the most challenging; their reluctance to mention their location and history added a level of difficulty that Bammer embraced with a fervour bordering on the fanatic. As a result she found these jobs the most rewarding, at least at a personal level. The system remained the same though - Jay took the requests, he'd give the information about what he needed to Bam, and she'd find it, then hand that information to Jay to take whatever action was requested.

It was all very lucrative. Additional income came via the experiment, which in the end caused so much damage. The problem, apparently, was that the impact of the experiment couldn't be adjusted. There were no partial exposures; it was an all or nothing affair. There was scope perhaps for further development, but it became clear that the trial outcomes were too drastic. As this became all too clear, Bammer stated that she refused to continue the project "...for any money, or for any reason".

She backed her refusal by returning all payments she had received for the project.

Her distress began as soon as the first few subjects entered the trial. The ensuing exposure to the program made the subjects revile themselves to such a degree that they took their lives, or performed unbelievably painful procedures upon themselves. All of them died within a very short space of time.

Because no-one ever saw Bammer, and as she was still responding to emails, no-one gave her decision to stop the project much thought.

When Jay found her she had already carved a latticework of slices in both her legs, some deep enough to require stitching. The repairs to these slices and stabs had been carried out with surprising competence by Bammer.

She was barcly hanging on though. Every mirror in her apartment destroyed, every reflective surface smeared with blood or food.

Jay had no choice but to take her to for a psyche assessment. Thankfully, Bammer didn't resist. She knew she needed help.

She didn't leave the hospital for three months. The medical staff couldn't reverse the damage the experiment had done. Drugs seemed to help to a degree, but left her almost completely vegetative. So a system of coping mechanisms was put together and the doctors said that for as long as she managed to adhere to them she'd be okay. This turned out to be true – with a lot of discipline she *was* okay, just.

Because Jay and Bammer had become so close during the time they worked together, Jay stayed by Bam's side throughout her hospitalisation and during the months that followed. In the early weeks after her release, he tried to stay with her around the clock, often sleeping in her bed and holding her while the demons circled. They never became lovers though. After Bam returned to work, the relationship stalled. It didn't fall away, it just didn't go any further, not for want of trying on Jay's behalf it seemed. Bammer was just too involved in the work to get connected to him, particularly when the work took him away, at times for months at a stretch.

That was her excuse at least. Jay figured it went deeper than that, that her almost pathological shyness locked her into being involved in things she could actually control.

Like the data.

"So, why did you split up - if you that's what you call it?" I asked.

"I was asked to perform a task that I wasn't comfortable with," said Jay

"What task was that?"

"To murder someone," he replied.

# 26.

"I hate myself for it. Sometimes the information that I had Belinda secure for me only required that I supply the whereabouts of an individual that someone was looking for. Belinda called these 'HW Data Searches'."

"HW?"

"Habits and Whereabouts. In these transactions I was only the mediator, keeping the parties apart. It protected Belinda, because it meant that I could control the level of contact she would be exposed to. It wasn't until she made a comment about the subject of one of our assignments dying in a horrific car accident that I became suspicious. I did my own crosschecking of our other HW's and found that six out of ten of them were dead. One was outright murdered, the others all found death in freak accidents."

I nodded, again not liking where the conversation was going – we were walking in the neighbourhood of our current safe house, it was early evening.

"I didn't tell her," he looked at the ground and shoved his hands in his pockets. "I should have, but didn't." He took a few more steps before continuing, "So when this offer came through and because of the sizable fee being offered, just out of sheer curiosity she decided to find out what had happened to the previous subjects of her searches. She did her own checks and found out the truth - we had been murdering people. I mean we didn't cut the brake lines or load the gun, but we had blood on us nonetheless."

He took a deep breath.

"Belinda didn't take it very well, I was worried that it might be enough to end her, but it didn't. It was something she understood, she knew how she was involved and what it meant, and she knew how to end her involvement as well. She sent me an email telling me that she didn't ever want to see me again, then set off a string of code that bored into the heart of the main servers that involved The Cult, and digitally nuked them. The data had been backed up, but it took months to restore all the files. In that time she simply disappeared."

Jay looked at me like I had brought her back from the dead.

"She was impossible to find. I even tried using some of the other tracking geeks, she was just… gone. Until now, I thought she might have unravelled after the work of disrupting The Cult had been done, but here you are, not only telling me she is alive, but holding some of her digital brilliance in your laptop."

"If I could make the link work I'd send her your regards. But even with your masterful stoke of supplying me with a cable, it seems that I can broadcast and access the Internet but I can't receive email."

"She's probably been under fire since your liberation from the Velcro chair. Shutting one of the information pipes helps to shore things up. Or at least that's how she used to explain it to me."

*****

The morning after the walk, and the deep and concerning conversation that it delivered, I set about sending more messages to Bam. I wasn't sure if she was even getting them, but I sent them anyway.

The messages I sent were brief, I mentioned nothing other than that there had been trouble, that while I was still in danger, I had gained the help of someone and we were okay.

I told her that I was going to withdraw the entire amount from the debit cards in the next day or so.

I also told her I missed her.

Jay's stories helped me understand his experiences with The Cult, but at the same time our talks spoke volumes about Bammer. The days it took to extract all the information from Jay told me more about her than the months of time she and I had spent together.

I missed Bammer. Maybe there would be a chance for... something. I told myself that a lot of conditions would need to be put in place and given the people we had become, we'd need rules and boundaries.

I rubbed at my face. What was I thinking? I needed to stay focussed. I needed to deal with what happened to Her, but instead of avenging Her death, I had found myself on the run from the very people that probably put out the contract to kill her in the first place.

I wondered whether I was suffering from a serious case of absence making the heart grow fonder, and whether the stress of the situation was making me want to fall back into my usual holding pattern: hide in a room with a computer and an internet connection.

While holed up at the motel, I at least felt like there was something being achieved. I was comforted by the discipline that involved in a process that had to be adhered to. All the moving about and the safe houses with the clandestine cat-and-mouse act Jay and I were playing felt like the control had been taken away from me.

Not being able to know if Bam was getting my emails and texts only made me feel more isolated.

*****

"Send her an email, or a text, or both, asking for her to put an ad in the classified section of The Guardian online or something," said Jay. "Maybe a personal ad, at least then you'll know if she is receiving."

"Excellent idea regarding an entry in the personals - any specifics you are looking for in a new companion?" I asked.

Jay laughed.

"Oh, I don't know, how about…must like cats and travel?" he said.

I sent Bam an email, then backed it up with a text message.

"We really should be considering what we are going to do next," I said.

It had been two weeks and I was certain that our trail had at least cooled enough to begin to forming a plan.

Jay said, "That depends on what you are trying to achieve. If you are still hell-bent on exacting some kind of retribution for Her death, you really only have a couple of choices. Continue to hang around here and utilise the safe house system, or go home, regroup, and work out a new strategy."

I had been thinking almost exactly the same thing.

Jay continued, "Me? If I were you I'd consider the latter. Don't get me wrong, you can stay moving between these worker houses for years, it's a huge network and the likelihood of actually running into anyone is extremely low. But for now, your face is marked here in London. It's going to take some time before your little attempt at infiltration is moved lower in the 'things that need to be resolved' stack. That time could be months, years, or decades away."

I had forgotten the effort it took to get this far, and in all the excitement and stress of hiding, and then remaining hidden, I had failed to remember that not only had I been marked in real life, my online persona would now be dead. I would have to start all over again. Months and months of work, gone.

Jay was still talking, "… at least that way you'd have a level of safety."

"I'm sorry, what was that last part?" I asked, forcing myself to concentrate on the present.

"I said that at least if you go home you can get to work on altering any records they might have on you. There's likely to be a lot of photos and footage from the gathering that will need to be altered or removed entirely in order to start rebuilding your identity. Or create a new one."

"I'm not sure that I'm ready to give up," I said.

"It's not about giving up, it's about realising what you are up against. You took a massive gamble showing up at a gathering, even larger when you came into contact and spoke at length to that pond scum, Martin. Come to think of it you might actually have to alter what's left of your existing identity to help you with future projects *and* you might have to take on an entirely new identity. A clean sheet, so to speak, would allow you to do your work unhindered by the inconveniences a team of crack programmers no doubt have in store for you once they get a handle on your signature."

Jay was right.

As the weight of what he had said settled, I knew that whatever was to come, whatever retribution I was looking at visiting upon Her murderer, it was going to be years away.

"You look like you need a drink," he said.

"I think you are right," I replied as I sank in to my chair.

Jay disappeared into one of the rooms of the house we were staying in, and returned with a large warm coat which he tossed to me along with a t-shirt with Bob Marley emblazoned across it.

"Put them on," he said.

"What, I have to get dressed up to go to the refrigerator now?"

"Nope," he said as he again disappeared into another room, this time the one slept in the night before, "I think we can chance a night out. There's a pub near here that does the best pie and chips a fugitive could ask for, and it's the kind of place that people can blend into. Provided you have a drink in your hand no one will ask any questions."

I changed into the t-shirt. Just as I was done, he returned and threw me the Rasta hat he had been wearing the night I first met him.

"Here, you'll need this too," he said. "Can't have you roaming about half disguised." Once more, he ducked into his room, appearing five minutes later wearing similar clothes. "Don't want you to think you have to get up and sing 'One love' all on your own if it comes on the jukebox."

"You sure this is a good idea?"

"Yeah, we need it. We've been moving around so much that I think we can chance a few hours out and about. Besides, the pub I'm talking about is just up the road, you could almost hit it with a rock from here."

"Right then, we will need some kind of alternative names…," I suggested.

"You might need an alternative name, I'm sticking with my own," he said, laughing.

"Alright, but I'm changing mine, what about something like 'Earth-child', how's that?" I suggested.

"Sounds sickening, I'll just call you EC, or maybe E for short, should we need to introduce ourselves to new and exciting people. Which we might as well. I need someone else to talk to. I mean, you're good company, but you really do keep up on your serious pills don't you?" he said, teasing.

I threw a cushion at him. "I was comfortable in my Velcro fitted chair before YOU came along throwing yourself in to the breach and all that," I then performed an extremely poor impersonation of him bursting into the room. "Stand back, for I am Jay, hand over your prisoner."

"Oh, OH, that's how it was, was it? Last time I do that for anyone," he said, laughing.

"That's exactly how it was. Was just about to get a scalp exfoliation and everything…"

We left the house and headed to the pub.

# 27.

"You need to get up."

I tried ignoring the voice, hoping it would just go away.

It didn't.

"You need to get up. Right now."

Something had prodded me awake. I felt awful.

I pulled the cover over my head.

"Fuck. Off," I said, hoping that I wouldn't have to take more drastic action. The effort involved in speaking those two words was almost too great.

"I am not kidding. You need to drag yer arse out of bed."

"Jay, you sound like Milke," I said as I pulled the covers back down, only to find myself not staring at Jay trying to sound like Milke, but Milke himself.

"Wait. What, where…?" I said as I sat up, the sudden movement causing my head to feel like it was impaled on something sharp and rusted.

"You need to get up, we will be leaving in an hour," he said. Impassive as ever.

"Wait," I called to Milke as he was leaving, "Where's Jay?"

"Making you breakfast. You don't half look like shit," he said and walked out into the main room. The smell of bacon suddenly wafted toward me.

I took some time to make my way to the kitchen, a catastrophic hangover making it hard for me to move or think. The memories of last night came flashing back, albeit fleetingly - a haze of beer and shots of various liqueurs were making their presence felt, along with a barely remembered kebab, or pizza, and at least one kind of curry.

"Morning, Sunshine," said Jay. He looked fine, the bastard.

"Jay, we are in hiding, you don't need to shout – you'll attract people. I don't want to deal with people."

"Here," he said and placed a cup of coffee down in front of me, along with a plate of bacon and eggs.

I nursed the coffee cup in two hands. The plate of food I pushed away.

Jay, resplendent in cooking apron, put his hands on his hips and said in the most motherly voice he could manage, "You don't like my cooking do you? I slave away, and what do I get…"

"It doesn't bother me none," said Milke as he swooped upon my plate. I reached over and took a length of bacon from it, and Milke watched it leave his newly acquired breakfast like a cat watching a feather toy being waved in front of it.

"That was brave," said Jay "He's done people in for less than that."

"It was my breakfast!" I said, and immediately regretted raising my voice.

"Mine now" said Milke, and moved his chair further away, positioning his arm so as to guard against any further infractions upon his food space.

I moved my cup over and placed my forehead on the table, the cool melamine felt therapeutic and I wondered why I hadn't thought of it earlier.

"You really are suffering aren't you?" asked Jay, who, if he was hung-over at all, was masking the experience successfully.

"Don't gloat, it doesn't... oh just don't gloat," I said, the melamine reflecting the words. "What are you doing here, Milke?"

"Having breakfast," came Milke's reply, between shovelled mouthfuls of food.

I sighed, both Jay and Milke laughed.

"He's here because he is going to drive us to France. News has come to hand that would suggest that we would be better off getting the hell out of England. News from Belinda, so it must be serious."

He tossed a copy of the Guardian on to the table, it slid to rest next to me, and I turned to see if I could read it without having to raise my head. Trying to focus at such close range caused my brain to ache in new and exciting ways, so I sat up and immediately gripped my head, resolving to be more considerate of my weakened state in the future.

"What am I looking at?" I asked.

"It's open at the page, personals, third entry down in the second column," Jay came and reached over my shoulder to point at the ad in question.

*Tired of finding the wrong people? Get out of where you are and come visit France. Spontaneous ex-pat living abroad has room available, free of charge. Come to a new country and start afresh! No danger, no commitments. Just see where things go. Must be articulate and like puzzles/Thai food /pizza and floor picnics in front of bad TV. Apply immediately, tomorrow will be too late!*

"How do you know it's Bammer?" I asked.

"How could you think it's not?" he replied.

"Hardly a reason to back its authenticity, don't you think?" I said, even though I didn't feel like it could be anyone but Bammer.

"Phone the number," said Milke, finished shovelling his food he had taken to wiping his plate with a bread roll.

"Good idea," said Jay. "She's hardly going to offer a secure number to call, she'll probably bomb it once you've contacted her."

"I'm going to vomit," I said.

"BOMB it, I said "bomb it". She'll nuke the number to stop any tracking, although you could wait a while. The amount of calls and texts she is getting is probably sending her mad," Jay grinned at the thought.

"Fine, is that a secure phone? Or at least secure enough?" I asked pointing at the phone on the wall.

"It is, but it doesn't really matter. That number is an English number, she's probably got it routed via Australia by way of Nepal, there'll be no tracing it either way."

I got up and walked slowly to the receiver and dialled the number.

*"Hi you've reached Bel,"* It was definitely Bam's voice, more chirpy than I had ever heard her before, *"If you're responding to the ad, thanks. Just leave a message after the beep and I'll get back to you."*

"Hi, yes I'd like to come and stay. I have been considering my next life step, so why not France? I will keep in contact. Thanks for your offer. Have been away too long, looking forward to…," there was another beep, and then the call disconnected.

"Shit," I said and hit redial, it didn't connect, so I tried again.

A new message had been left in place of the one I had just heard, short and chilling.

*"Leave now, they have found you. I'll assist where I can. Text visa locations and requirements. Your phone has been blocked but will work in short bursts in other countries. Go now."*

"Bammer says we have to go, and we have to go now."

"Right then, through the chunnel to the land of wine and cheese then," said Milke.

"No wine and cheese for me. Well, at least not today," I said.

Within the hour we were in the car driving away from the safe house, and heading toward Folkstone and the Channel Tunnel.

*****

At the train station, we decided to split up. Jay and I would buy tickets separately, while Milke took care of the car.

We would either meet on the train or at the other end, in Coquelles. How we determined to get out of France was still a mystery, but we figured we would have a better chance of resolving that once there.

After purchasing a ticket, I made my way to the boarding platform, keeping my head down when passing anyone that looked official. I tried to blend into the crowd, not sure about my new black beanie or my long black duffle coat flapping gently as I moved about.

I found a place on the platform not too far from the entry gate, but far enough to make it look like I wasn't waiting for someone and bided my time by pretending to read a newspaper.

Jay was wearing jeans, a branded sports t-shirt, a pair of running-trainers and looked every part the fashion victim as he came through the gate. He took five steps in my direction when a large man stepped out in front of him. Jay stepped to the side to try move around the newcomer, but the larger man kept up with the dance, making it obvious he wasn't going to let him past. Jay turned without so much as a glance at me, and made to move in the opposite direction. Another man stepped forward, again barring his way. Long black coats and sunglasses making both assailants look like something from a made-for-TV spy flick.

Jay made a break for it but the black coated men were too fast and had him pinned against the wall in no time. In short order he was cuffed and marched off the platform with a guard either side of him.

I was alone.

Jay was in trouble, but there was nothing I could do about it as the doors opened on the train carriages, the station staff indicating those on the platform should board.

I had no choice. "No matter what happens, get on that train. If one of us gets caught, the others have to keep on. If they are watching the place, there will be too many to try some daring raid like Camden, just keep your head down and keep on," Jay had said.

I hated it, but still got on the train and did everything I could to try to remain calm. As the train pulled away from the station I settled a little, but only until panic rose again as the ticket warden came through to check that his passengers were seated and that they had all their paperwork in order.

Thankfully he only took the shortest of glances at my ticket and passport, then hurried along.

The trip itself was singularly uneventful, but I was still hungover, and concerned that if Milke had also been detained, I would be on my own. Hadn't we done everything right? We certainly didn't stand out, and yet people were waiting for us at the station. Why hadn't they just nabbed us as we entered the place? All I could do was hope that Milke got through and that I would have at least one ally once off the train.

*****

In France, I tried to time my leaving the train so didn't place me as the first face out the door, while also avoiding being the last. I just figured that being in the middle of a crowd was safer.

Milke was nowhere to be seen, but we had discussed that we'd meet him and the car near the terminal, so it was no surprise that he wasn't on the platform.

No-one appeared to be following me, but 'shaking off a potential hidden assailant' wasn't anything that had been included in my presentations to prospective employers. To blend into the background I had decided to take on the persona of someone who was moderately busy, certain of where they were going and comfortable with the bustling of those around me.

What I desperately didn't want to show was that I was almost sure that the every secret service agent billeted in a 30 kilometre radius from the terminal had decided to do some private-investigator work on the side.

And that they were all in the station.

All looking for me.

# 28.

I had been to Paris once before on business, but that was the limit of my travels in France. Like many business tourists, my memory of that visit was one of an airport-to-hotel transfer, a conference, and an afternoon on a bus to go and see a famous tower and an arch or two.

Having just extricated myself from the station, I had none of those grandiose landmarks to act as a guide, just a rough map and a detailed verbal description of the meeting point floating around in my fuzzed brain.

The meeting point was to be the car park at a shopping mall near the Parc de la Rouge Cambre – a small green-space area nearby. A couple of French phrases, halting and clumsily exchanged with random people, along with a deep desire to get away from the station pushed me further into the surrounding area. With relief, I finally spotted the mall, and my pace quickened.

I recognised Milke's car immediately. We had discussed how to find the car given that we didn't know how busy the carpark would be. The answer was simple: Milke would park as close as practical to the corner of the car park farthest away from the entrance, the theory being that people would generally park as close to the entrance as possible, leaving the more remote parking areas free for Milke's use. It sounded too simple when we discussed it, and I was slightly shocked that our plan had worked.

I had the panicky feeling of foreboding; expecting that at any moment, from behind every car, someone would leap out then drag me, kicking, into a large black van to be taken somewhere and chained to a wall next to Jay. If indeed there was enough of Jay left to be chained to a wall.

The car was still idling as I approached. The weather was cool, and for all Milke's gruff nature he did like his comforts. No doubt he was keeping the heater running. I was glad he was in the car, it meant that he hadn't been accosted at the station.

Most of all, I was glad that I wasn't the only one here. I barely knew the guy, but he seemed solid, if somewhat slow on the uptake – at least when it came to anything beyond pints of beer and darts.

Milke's car was parked next to a large rubbish skip, the gentle waft of the bin reaching me as I approached from the rear and along the drivers' side of the car. I picked up my pace as I passed his window. One look through the broken glass made my imaginary pursuers become more solid, more *present,* as my feet crunched on the pebbled and shattered shards.

Milke was dead, his trademark sunglasses hung from one ear, the side of his head closest to the window had been pulped by whatever weapon that was used, leaving the wet matter of his brain fluffed and falling like some macabre soft-centred treat.

I only glanced, but the damage was so devastating and extensive, a moment was all that was needed. Had I stayed longer I would have been drawn into the finality of Milke's last moments. It would have been too much.

All I knew was that I had to get away.

*****

There was an outlet store that opened directly onto the carpark. Nothing fancy, and festooned with red banners that didn't need the benefit of translation – it's the kind of place that would seem to always have some kind of sale on, it's a universal department store experience. It wasn't going to be the height of fashion, but whatever they had that would alter my appearance would do.

Rummaging through the sale racks, I searched for clothes that didn't stand out, but were obviously different to the ones I was wearing. I settled on a grey coat similar to the black one I had been wearing and a black jumper, then paid for my clothes and, to the salesperson's astonishment, went immediately back into the changing room and put them on, leaving my old coat hanging on the hook in the cubicle like a body left swinging on the gallows. As I stuffed remaining gear into my travel bag I realised that of all the things on my person, my backpack was the most likely to be recognised, no matter what clothes covered the body that was toting it.

Thankfully the store had a sizable array of backpacking equipment, so I selected one that looked inconspicuous enough and told the sales person I wished to test its capacity. I emptied my existing travel sack and placed all the contents into the new pack. The sales guy helped me on with the pack, I paid, and left, heading back toward the terminal.

For the first time since entering France I turned on my phone. Almost immediately, I got a signal and a text from Bammer.

*No good coming home. Not safe to fly. Safety here compromised. Am coming to meet you. Hire a car. Go to Budapest. All visas active. Text when you arrive. No communication otherwise. Bad times. They've found us.*

Budapest. A plan. Even without the physical presence of Bammer, the idea that she was coming made me feel a little less isolated.

The hire-car would be a good thing. Hopefully, Bam would have access to the tunnel to hollow out the contract I'd have to sign, and of course change the destination in the rental firm's data base.

Bammer had probably chosen Budapest as somewhere to meet because the massive dossier she had on me noted that I had travelled there before. Actually, I had travelled frequently to Budapest. More so during the early stages of my consulting career, and, in later years, She would come with me. We had wandered the streets together, drinking coffee and eating as much homemade goulash as we could stand. After dark, we would stalk the back streets to find hidden nightclubs and bars that were shut away behind nondescript doors that opened inward to a world of extraordinary music, and sweat, and bump and grind, all performed in commandeered apartments and car parks.

It was a place I could easily hide. I had some friends there as well; or, at least people I knew well enough to ask a favour or two.

I needed a car. To get a car I had to go back to the terminal. I briefly considered taking Milke's car, but quickly discounted the thought. Apart from having to deal with Milke's pulped head, his car was likely to be marked and geo-tagged by now. I'd get far enough out of town to be away from prying eyes before they would simply swoop in and it would all be over.

It had to be a hire car, so I steeled myself for the re-entry into the terminal by running a constant pep talk around and around in my head. Cautiously I neared the station and used the zebra crossing once the road was clear enough. Keeping my eyes down I watched each stripe as I stepped over it, the paint's raised, ragged edges scarring the road.

Once across the carriageway I looked up and saw the rental car stands directly ahead. Rather than head directly for them, even though every fibre of my being was telling me to run, I held back. It was the obvious place for someone to go, and although I was out of my depth, I decided to try to blend in to the crowd in order to take stock of what could be seen.

A coffee stand had set up on the path approaching the terminal entrance, its single barista seemingly superhuman in his ability to supply the caffeine demands from the passing crowd. I waited my turn, and then ordered a café latte; if the guy was at all offended with my butchering his language as I made my order, he gave no sign.

I added sugar to my steaming paper cup and took a sip – but it became apparent that no amount of sugar would help whatever it was that was in my cup. It might have been coffee, but it was awful. It was so bad that for a moment I almost forgot the predicament I found myself in and pondered briefly on how a country so proud of its culinary excellence could get coffee so very, very wrong.

Still, I sipped and took the time between grimaces to see if I could notice anyone that looked suspicious among the many waiting in the open areas around the terminal. I couldn't be sure, paranoia was creeping in, so rather than finding anyone who looked like they wished to do me harm, I found it was easier to spot the few I thought least likely to pull a weapon on me.

There was still an inch of coffee left in the cup, but feeling that I had struggled enough, I tossed the remnants into the can next to the cart. I couldn't afford to wait any longer, I had been exposed for long enough, so I approached the terminal again and plunged into the gloom.

The choice of car company was an easy one; the counter I found myself at won my business primarily because I had an account already. As a result, there was no requirement to use a credit card for the security deposit. I handed the cash over for two weeks of car rental on the cheapest car that was fuelled up and ready to go.

Fifteen minutes later I was leaning on the hood of my new car, signing the last of the forms that were required before I could quit the car park and drive across Europe to the safety that I hoped could be found in Budapest.

Waving goodbye to the rental attendant, I moved out of the parking space and drove to the exit to wait for the boom gate to let me go. Three people passed in front of the car on the other side of the gate. Two black suited men, dark glasses on their neatly shaved faces. The third was busy talking in fast spurts in to his cell phone, one arm held up in a sling.

Martin.

The boom gate opened and I eased my foot onto the accelerator pedal, calmly indicating and turning in the opposite direction to the one in which the three men were heading. The gate felt like a flood release as the car park emptied me out on to the road, distance already put between me and my enemy.

# 29.

I spent the day driving carefully and doing my best to not stick out. I obeyed the speed limits, smiled at petrol station attendants and did my best to look relaxed even though my heart would often be beating at an alarming rate.

A small bed and breakfast near the France/Belgium border was my first stop. Then and an early start in order to spend the day getting through Belgium, finally stopping at again at dusk to stay at a small beer house that had lodging out back. I took my meal in my room and came out after the dinner rush to sit at the bar and enjoy a couple of drinks. Anxiety took over and forced me to leave just as I finished the first glass. The barman, rightly seeing that something was wrong, followed me out to my room.

"Is there anything I can get you?" he asked, his English was excellent.

"No, I'm just tired."

"Just thought I had better check," he said. "It's hard travelling on your own, I'll be back in a moment."

"No, really, don't go to any…," I said, but he was waving at me over his shoulder.

He returned with a bottle of wine and one glass, a small fruit platter and a TV remote control.

"We usually charge extra for television, but we don't have many staying tonight, doesn't seem worth holding out for another euro or two." He bustled into the room and placed the cheese platter on the single side table in the room, already marked with coffee rings and the odd cigarette burn on its otherwise clean surface. He put the bottle and wine glass on the floor next to an old but comfortable-looking arm chair, then poked at the remote control until the television came on, the volume low.

Handing me the remote he said, "All on the house. Sometimes you just need wine, cheese, and television. Goodnight."

*****

I didn't see him again until breakfast, when I handed over the empty cheese platter and the glass.

"Thank you. You were absolutely right."

"I know I was. Never wrong," he said, indicating I should seat myself at a table by the window where, in short order, coffee and a large breakfast of sausages, eggs, and mushrooms, along with a half loaf of bread was parked in front of me.

The barman came to join me with what looked like a huge bowl of porridge. A woman, who I assumed to be his wife, attended to an elderly couple sipping tea and eating dry toast.

"Thanks again, I…"

"No need, say nothing more." he said.

"Okay. Anyway, I probably should get a start on this mountain of food you've put in front of me," I said.

I picked up my fork and perused the plate. The food looked too good to eat, and was so neatly arranged that it looked like it had been taken directly from the pages of a cookbook that specialised in rustic cuisine.

The owner pointed his spoon at each of the objects on my plate and explained where they had come from. All of it came from within a five minute walk from where we were sitting.

"You'll need to keep your strength up," he said.

"How so?" I asked, more edge in my voice than I would have liked.

"I can just tell. Little things like when you paid for your room in advance you made a point of saying that you didn't require a receipt. Suggests that you are obviously not here on a business trip, or you would be paying by card or requiring a receipt to recover cash from your company."

"You are right, I'm not here on business."

"Then, instead of wandering around our quiet little town, you went immediately to your room, ate in your room, then survived for just one drink out here before rushing back."

"I could just be an anxious person."

"You could, but you don't seem to be naturally anxious."

"I am becoming more anxious now…"

He laughed, put his spoon down and raised his hands in mock submission.

"Please don't let our conversation ruin your breakfast, I'd hate to think all those farmers went to so much effort to fill that plate only to have you leave it barely touched."

He sounded genuine, so I tentatively went back to poking at my food.

"I don't mean to pry at all, I was only making observations, and in my showing you how I came to my assumption I have been delayed from telling you the most important part. That my knowing you are moving around quietly is a good thing, it means that should anyone come asking for you, I won't know who you are. Or at least I will tell them I don't know who they are talking about."

His face turned a little sombre as he continued, "I know the feeling, I truly do. It is how I ended up here. I wanted to disappear, so one day I did. If it wasn't for many people who in their own way assisted me the way I will assist you if I have to, I would be somewhere else entirely. I am simply paying the favour back, it is all I can do to say thanks."

My appetite returned and I attacked my plate with gusto. The owner smiled.

"So, back to my original statement, you will need your strength. If I were you, I wouldn't stop today except for fuel until you find somewhere to stay for the evening. If you are going through Germany then I suggest that you take your time." he waited briefly to see if I would indicate whether that was part of my plan or not, I might have flinched a little but he went on nonetheless: "Meander along the smaller roads where possible, just tell your GPS to take you via scenic routes."

I nodded. It had already occurred to me to not be so hasty about covering ground so quickly.

"I'll have my wife make a lunch hamper for you so you don't have to stop anywhere… for today at least."

"Thanks," I said after swallowing another fork-full of bacon.

"No need, as I said, I am only repaying a favour."

He rose, picked up his porridge-bowl, and departed through the door behind the bar, where I supposed the kitchen must be. My plate was empty, and the owner's wife took some fending off so that she didn't immediately fill it again. I said no to the food, but yes to more coffee, which she brought to the table with a smile.

Another day would be welcome at this little safe harbour, with its warm, timber-clad interior. However, while haste was to be avoided, there was still a timeframe to be worked toward. Bammer would be getting closer, and so I had to be moving onward as well, particularly if a circuitous route were to be taken. I vowed to return one day and walk around the quiet little town, and hoped that my path didn't lead me too far away from a small part of the world that was filled with kind words and cheese platters.

*****

An hour later I was on the road. The tarmac was wet with morning dew, but drying where the traffic had already been as I engaged in slow and indulgent drive to the limits of the town while committing as much of it to memory as I could. The old cottages and bridges seemed calm and pretty; a stark counterpoint to my flight across the country. My lunch was suitably nestled on the passenger seat and it smelled delicious, as the delicacies prepared for me wafted through its tea-towel wrapping.

Outside the village, rather than just gun for the border on the highway, I tried to run parallel to it as best as I could, popping out on to the main road to cross into Germany. Then it was back to searching out the secondary roads that would keep me hidden.

The rest of the day was spent adhering to the plan – moving slowly but surely toward Austria, only stopping once for fuel and then to eat the lunch that had so lovingly been prepared for me. Without leaving the car I ate my little feast, and with crumbs in my lap I drove on until the light began to fail, and it was time to stop. Testing a theory that had been playing in my mind for the afternoon, I decided to take the first right-hand turn off the main street of the next town, and stop at the first place that looked like it could give me a room for the night. The only contingency being that, whatever lodging it happened to be, it didn't have the look that suggested a guest would the need to share their room with an infestation of rodents.

The plan worked. A pleasant sign stating 'Guest house' swung lightly on its chains as I pulled in to the small parking space, tyres crunching on the gravelled allotment.

The lodgings were not as homely as the previous night, but it was off the main road, so as far as I was concerned all the boxes in my mental list of shelter requirements were ticked.

The owner saved me the issue regarding the receipt by gratefully accepting cash payment and not producing one.

This time, I complained of headache and asked to be shown to my room. He ushered me to a quiet, clean room and told me that a meal could be brought to me if I would rather.

It all worked out perfectly, my feigned illness deflating anything that could be considered suspicious behaviour. Exhausted, I went to bed after the food had been delivered and consumed, and slept like the dead, waking refreshed and feeling ahead of the game.

After a shower and breakfast I found a petrol station and then continued on my winding route. A new sense of enthusiasm crept into my psyche as the distance between me and Budapest became less, and made me hope the distance between me and my pursuers was becoming greater.

This is not to say that I had grown cavalier in my approach; every car in the rear view still held the potential for violence, but the sense of progression toward an end game at least allowed me to acknowledge the scenery as I twisted and turned through the rural European back-roads. Tiny villages and larger towns came and went. Farmland, no doubt tended year round by the landholders, giving away little as to what it would yield in return for the hard work ploughed into it. Beautiful mountains, snow-capped and fresh from a postcard, there was magic here. The magic of simple everyday life.

I'd catch myself in this dream-like state and then immediately snap back to the present, for while I was confident, I was still very much aware that *they* would be on the lookout. A feeling that ebbed and flowed, often a sharp breath would announce the surprise of a previously unnoticed car behind mine. I'd hold my breath and then exhale, the feeling leaking from me at the same time the pursuing car put on its indicator and pulled into a side street.

Traffic cameras were blocked by a raised hand and often the added security of the sun visor pulled down. I stuck to large breakfasts bolstered by petrol-station snacks throughout the day. For the most part, the journey was pleasant. Thought the moments of panic were crippling.

# 30.

Passing through Austria and on into Hungary offered no more challenge than travelling through Germany and I made good time in spite of my winding path. I ditched the car on arriving in Budapest, and took the opportunity to go underground and use the rail system. All tickets were cash only, and the odd manner in which each line is operated by a different company was familiar enough to create a feeling that some kind of foundation was forming - a safe base in which to fortify for what ever was to happen next.

Budapest is one of my favourite towns. There is an honesty in it that is hard to find in other world-capitals. It is brutal at times, something that I was reminded of while passing a homeless man in the middle of one of the subway tunnels, commuters all but walking over him to get to their train. But at other times the artistry and humanity of its citizens is breathtaking. The crumbling city was slowly being restored, the cracked façades refurbished rather than being replaced, small camera stores sold old cameras, and coffee shops served great coffee as buses that were connected to overhead electric lines weaved their impossible way along busy streets.

I stayed in a small hostel near one of the Universities in Pest. I'd stayed there before, although not for a very long time. It was very much a backpacker's hostel, but also offered private rooms that were clean, secure, and most importantly for me, buried in an apartment block. My preferred room was downstairs adjoining the courtyard near the entrance to the block, and I was glad that it was available.

The owner, Csaba, greeted me as an old friend and introduced me to the new live-in managers. The itinerant nature of hostel workers meant that while these were the new managing staff, they were the third set of 'new staff' since the last time I was here. Even though they were far removed from the couple I remembered, they were still as enthusiastic and hell-bent on partying as the previous managers. I got the feeling that if I wasn't so preoccupied with my current situation there would be a blistering hangover waiting for me within the next sixteen hours.

To circumvent any invitations that might be in the offing for a campaign-like pub crawl, I used my tried-and-true headache ploy in order to extricate myself from any social requirements, and following the routine, asked whether some food could be brought to my room. "Like a sandwich or something," I suggested.

The request caused Csaba to ask good naturedly whether I "thought this was the fucking Hilton", but nonetheless sent one of the backpackers down with my required snack.

Once settled, I turned the phone on again and began to tap out a message to Bam, when it in turn vibrated and then pinged that a message had just been delivered.

*I have been delayed. Am nearby. Looking forward to seeing you. Will touch the cross on the bridge tomorrow and then will come directly to B-pest. Do not send your location. Leave phone off, turn on at the 6's. B. xx*

It was good to hear from her. I had certainly been well looked after by the strangers I had met in the last few days, but to have contact with someone I actually knew was refreshing. That she looked forward to seeing me was strangely comforting.

The message had a time stamp of 6.05am two days earlier, the section alluding to the cross on the bridge meant that she was intending to be in Prague the day after the message was sent. Or at least that is what I assumed. The cross on the bridge at Prague is the only reference I could think of.

That meant that Bam was likely to be in Budapest now. It was 2pm and I decided to adhere to Bam's instructions and turned the phone off again until 6pm.

I decided on an afternoon nap, feeling safe in my hidden apartment, the travels and stresses of the last few days finally catching up with me.

My eyes shut and I fell into a dead sleep until waking with a start at 6.30, scrambling for my phone and jabbing my thumb at the power button.

No messages blinked up on my screen so I went outside to make sure that my phone had access to every ounce of phone reception possible, coupled with an illogical idea that the strongest phone signal would make the potential of a message greater. It didn't and I stood in the tiled courtyard unsure of what to do next.

Csaba was standing on the balcony above.

"You look refreshed. Come up and enjoy some of the hospitality you've been missing for the last couple of years," he said.

"I really should be thinking more about food, rather than beer," I replied.

"How about both? It's goulash night – the backpackers are cooking, I am directing."

"That could be either a great thing or a bad thing," I said as I made my way toward the stairwell and up to the covered corridor leading to the little hostel.

*****

The group sitting around the common room of the hostel were a small bunch of wide-eyed and happy travellers in their early twenties, each one a microcosm of ego and attitude that was at odds with the bags of self-conscious worry that they had carried in their myriad packs through Europe. As most backpackers do during their new realisation adulthood and self-reliance, they set about masking their perceived personal short-fallings with bravado.

Csaba's place had always got the balance right, actively discouraging poor attitudes and passively reinforcing the edict by including all his guests in whatever crazy scheme he and his team had cooked up for the week's activities. No matter who walked though the front door, everyone was treated the same, and during their stay and would be imbued with a shared love or food and fun coupled with copious amounts of alcohol, if that was their thing.

Goulash night was typical of the hostel.

Various Hungarian delicacies had been placed in the common area by Csaba, and the travellers all took turns in attending the goulash-pot that was teetering on an archaic looking stove in the kitchen. Their job was to make sure the goulash was bubbling happily, with Csaba calling out instructions over the low counter that covered the vagaries of stirring velocity, and the difference between spatula and spoon and their attendant mixing properties.

Everyone had to take their turn, no matter what phase of some neo-political diatribe some of the more serious young folk were getting themselves into. When the timer went off, they had to go and tend to the pot. It was a process that went on for some time, until Csaba announced that the food was ready and began to serve up ladles of the spiced meaty stew.

A bell rang and Csaba looked up at the girl who was on duty as receptionist that evening, not that there was a reception to speak of, but someone had to greet new guests, and on goulash night Csaba always delegated that task to someone else.

The girl went, opened the door and then called out something in Magyar, Csaba got up and looked at me. As the oldest in the room, apparently that meant I was supposed to take charge, so I followed Csaba out to the landing to find him and the receptionist crouched next to a body, slumped on the weather-stained concrete.

It was Bammer.

# 31.

"Shit," I said.

"You know this girl?"

"Yes, yes I do. She was supposed to be contacting me to meet her."

"I tried to." she croaked.

She was a mess. It was dark so I couldn't tell how bad things were but she looked like she had been run over by a car. It turns out she had. Her arm was heavily bandaged and she was wearing a knee splint along with just about every size of sticking plaster across her face.

"Bam, what the fuck?" I said, shocked to see her at all, let alone in such a state.

"Take her down to your apartment, I will go back inside and tell my kids that everything is okay." He always referred to the backpackers as 'His' kids.

Csaba was angry, I couldn't blame him – the backpacker trade was hard enough as it was, the last thing any Hosteller needed was to have someone show up half dead in his common room.

The receptionist and I helped Bam down stairs and through the little courtyard to the apartment. An old woman who lived in one of the other apartments adjoining the courtyard opened her door and peered out, saw the three of us lurching toward my place and quickly thought better of speaking to us.

The receptionist opened the door while I supported Bam, assisted us through, then left immediately, leaving me to man-handle Bammer across the room.

I helped lay her down on the bed and turned the heating on.

"Oh Bam," I said, "You look awful."

"Told you, I TOLD you I was hideous," she said softly with a hint of a smile, maybe.

"Enough of that," I replied, and leaned down to kiss her on the forehead.

"But seriously, what on earth happened to you?" I asked.

"I took a wild guess that you would be here. Well not that wild, you really are a creature of habit, it made sense for you to come here, or at least it made sense to me."

I went to the small bar fridge and got her some of the orange juice I had purchased on the way from the station.

She sipped and made a face as the acid in the juice obviously sluiced through a wound inside her cheek, then put the glass down.

"I caught the train to Vienna, then Vienna to here. I had the feeling that someone had tried to contact me, in a bad way, in Prague. So I hired a car and then ditched it a couple of hours away at Brno and caught the Prague-Vienna train from there".

She looked like she was fading. I told her to wait until morning, she said she'd rather get it all done now.

"I got off the train here, left the station and was waiting to cross that intersection outside the main gate. Someone pushed me in front of a car that was trying to beat the red light. Luckily, the driver swerved and really only clipped me but still it was hard enough that I needed an ambulance and some time at the hospital."

"At least they discharged you early," I said.

"Discharged? Who said anything about a discharge?" she replied.

We both laughed.

"I've missed you Bam. I really have. I can't tell you how sorry I am about the way that I left."

"Oh, don't get all mushy on me now," she said, although I could see her eyes were a little wetter than before.

"I mean it Bam. And I mean it when I say I just don't know if I'm too broken. But I promise I'll try, that's all I can do.

"It's all I can promise too."

I kissed her again, this time on the lips, softly, careful of the split in the middle of her lip. Her mouth was soft, but swollen, and I could taste a mix of the orange juice and some kind of antiseptic. She reached up with her free hand and pulled me closer kissing me harder, sucking my bottom lip between her teeth.

She was crying.

"Please Bam, just rest."

"It's not that, I have to tell you something, something about my previous work…"

"It's okay, Jay told me," I said softly.

She pushed me away.

"Jay? You've met Jay?" she said, panicked.

"Yes, we met in Camden, he saved me from Martin."

"He SAVED you from Martin. Fuck. Fuck. Fuck. We have to go, we have to go now."

"You can't go anywhere Bam, look at you."

"We have to go. You have no idea how vulnerable we are, no fucking idea. He is the worst kind of person. The worst kind, he has no conscience. He is nothing but a machine."

"Are we talking about the same person?" I asked, obviously confused.

The door opened, the receptionist had failed to lock it.

It was Jay, and he was armed with a 9mm handgun, a silencer making it look almost comical, and unwieldy.

"Have you told him yet?" asked Jay, covering the area between us with the gun, ready to switch aim if either of us made a run for it.

"Have you?" he said.

Bammer had fallen to her knees, the splinted leg jutting out awkwardly.

"Jay, please don't."

She was sobbing.

"Jay, I don't know what the fuck is happening here. But put the gun down, how did you escape?"

Jay looked at me and smiled.

"Escape? It was a set up. Shame about poor Milke, but he wasn't down with the program it seems. I needed you to be free to move around. I needed you to lead me to her," he said, indicating Bam.

"Wait, what? What do you mean 'lead me to her?' " I said, the realisation that I had been little more than a pawn in this thing rained down upon me.

"You haven't told him have you?" he asked Bam again.

"Told me what?" I said turning to Bammer

She looked up at me and sobbed.

Jay again: "You had better tell him Belinda, tell him before I kill you, tell him about Her."

"Tell me what about Her? What do you know about Her?" I asked, anger beginning to fill me.

"I killed her," she said.

"You what?" I spat, "You fucking what?"

"That's not entirely true," said Jay. "I did the trigger pulling, so you can't take credit for that. What you can do is take the credit for finding her in the first place. It's why you struck up this friendship with your potential fuckbuddy here, isn't it?"

Bammer made a moaning noise, she might also have said something, but it wasn't intelligible.

The information all but floored me. Bammer had been hired to find Her. Jay had been in my yard, had stood next to the hammock while I went to make a drink. He'd walked up behind her and shot her, maybe with the gun he was trailing on us right now.

"Fucker."

"I was just doing the job I had been hired to do. Should have been done years before, but Bammer kept on saying she couldn't find Her. Turns out she had a crush on you and didn't want you to suffer, or something. I was all for shooting you too, but funds were put in place by someone else to keep you alive."

While the part about someone paying for my protection was beyond me, the history of our connection made some sense.

Bammer and I had become friends in an unusual way, we seemed to connect on so many levels and in a very short space of time. She seemed to know me or at least knew enough about me to engage in topics that I connected with.

My heart sank.

"What about the police officer? His family?"

"He started meddling in the case file, and with the added resources you had given him he was beginning to ask questions that jeopardised the system."

"But, his whole fucking family?" I said, taking a step toward him.

"Kinder in the long run. It's best to kill the whole herd. Better for the kids," he said, impassive, then pointed the gun at me stopping my advance. "Don't get yourself hurt now. You aren't on the list, but if I have to defend myself…"

I didn't retreat, I simply stood where I was, and tried to process what was happening. All the while Bammer sobbed, broken on the floor by the bed.

"Right, enough with the history lesson. I have a job to do, and it's sitting right there with mascara running into its cheek bandages," he said moving further into the room.

I moved toward Bammer who howled in terror and grabbed pitifully at my legs trying to hide behind them. I could feel her head resting against the back of my thighs, her busted arm holding on to a handful of my jeans, the other reaching out as if to deflect what was to come.

"I'm sorry, I'm so sorry… forgive me? Please. Please?" her voice from behind me.

"Sorry? Are you apologising to me?" asked Jay, taking another step toward us. "If you are, then it's been a long time coming. You abandoned me, you stupid girl. Now get out from behind there."

"Nooo, please nooo," she said, making herself as small as she possibly could.

"Right," he said, looking at me, "There's no other way for it then, I'm going to have to shoot her through your legs. I'll TRY not to hit you, but you know, you are kind of standing in front of my target."

"Who paid you to do this?" I asked.

"Oh no, this is free. Bitch left me hanging out to dry over that little job at The Beach. I was asked by the benefactor to resolve this little 'lack of co-operation' issue. So now I'm going to resolve it." He aimed the gun, Bammer had wet herself, I could smell the urine on the carpet, the warm fluid releasing the scent of years of pizza, beer and fucking from the old rug.

Three rapid fire shots, silenced, let fly.

'Phut, phut-phut.'

One grazed my thigh, the second was a mystery, the third coincided with the front of Jay's face blowing outward – warm pieces of flesh and salty cranial fluid covering my face, the projectile that caused the damage lodging in my shoulder.

A large man in a dark suit was standing in the doorway and he moved aside, so the man behind him could enter.

# 32.

"What have you brought to my hostel?" asked Csaba, looking nervous.

"Hopefully I'll be able to explain that one day. To be frank, it's a long story that I don't really have a handle on."

I was being tended to by a medic, although not one that was called in via any emergency number. He was part of the team that accompanied Martin to Budapest. As it happened the bullet that lodged near my shoulder was easily removed. The medic stitched me up and applied antibiotic powder from a plastic bottle, which he capped and then handed to me.

"Change and powder the wound three to four times a day. The stitches will have to stay in for a week to ten days, Google how to remove them." he said, then stood up and left.

Martin stepped over to Csaba and handed him a large wad of money, all in Hungarian Forints.

"Do not fear that this will affect anything, my team will clean up all the mess and pay for this room to be refurbished, no one will ever know what transpired here tonight. What I would suggest is that you take that cash and invite all your lodgers out on a bar-hopping expedition that will go down in the history of your hostel as the best night out that has ever been. We will be done with this mess tonight, and will send decorators during the next week to finish off. How does that sound to you?"

Csaba looked uncertain, but then considered the efficiency of the clean-up already in progress and decided that he could live with it. He looked at me in a manner that suggested that we had a lot of making up to do if I was considering a continuation of this friendship, then walked out into the courtyard, passing a guy with a trolley and a refrigerator coming in the other way.

"Makes getting the body out easier," said the guy wheeling the trolley.

Csaba nodded and increased the pace of his stride to the stairwell and all but ran up the stairs.

I went to the bathroom, wanting a shower to get the blood off me, but I also wanted to look after Bam, so I settled for a fast rinse instead. Lumps of Jay's flesh rolled underneath my palms as I wiped at my face, and I removed my jumper before bending over the shower space, turning the taps on so that I could at least get some of the blood and remains from my neck and chest.

I came out of the bathroom wearing a jumper worn a day too many, and carrying a bloodied towel. One of the 'team' reached out their hand and I instinctively handed over the towel. He took it, and placed it with other bloodied rags in a biohazard bag, an action that appeared so natural to him that I wondered how many of these clean-ups he had found himself involved in.

Bammer was seated on the floor, leaning in the corner made by the bed and the wall with her good knee drawn up to her chin. Martin was crouched in front of her, talking. I wasn't sure exactly what was being said, but it didn't sound accusatory or questioning, instead his voice sounded calm and reassuring.

He stood up as I arrived and Bam looked up at me briefly, her face crumpling before she put her head on her knee. Martin rested his hand on her head briefly.

"She never meant to do harm, you know, she didn't set out to do the things she has been blamed for. She was a researcher. Nothing more," said Martin.

"And how do you fit into this awful little picture? The last time I saw you we were involved in some kind of inquisition," I asked, not believing that we were yet out of danger.

"That was set up because we thought you were working for Jay. We knew that he was circling, but we had no idea what for. I guess he was trying to see if Belinda was still working, and if so, he whether he could use you to make a connection to her."

"He and I sat together at the gathering, you could have just have grabbed him."

"We weren't sure it was him, despite the fact that the two agents that we posted to that table you were sitting at have been following him around for a few months now. He must have known and allowed it to go on to strengthen his position. Once outside, he immobilised Pat, and then Lisa. They'll be okay though, once the casts come off."

He paused to direct one of the clean-up team, then continued:

"We grabbed at his association with you, and the fact that you had been asking a lot of questions, and exactly the right kinds of questions to get you noticed. We figured that you must be connected somehow. Your partner being murdered gave you reason to damage us or at least, damage the Black Angels."

"There doesn't seem to be that much difference between you," I said.

"The True Angels and the Black Angels? To the outsider, no. To us who are trying to build on the foundations of a new religion, the Black Angels do not serve us well at all. We know of their goings on, and we in no way support them, but overall we are powerless to stop them. Or at least we were. Things are changing even as we speak, the Black Angels are losing their romantic pull to those who are new to The Cult, their ways are becoming too... unpalatable."

"Fucking hell," I said, all of it sinking in slowly. Jay meeting me at the door and directing me to his table. The weak 'battery acid'. I shook my head, and rubbed at the bridge of my nose with my good hand.

"I think that's enough for now..."

"Wait, I need to know why She was murdered," I said, looking up again.

"Belinda is best placed to tell you that. Let me just add that she really had no knowledge of what was going to be done with the information she found, not until later. While she might have started the ball rolling, someone else finished the search, allowing Jay to catch up on his work. Her mistake was thinking that no one else could decipher such data. Seems she was wrong."

I turned to look at Bam. She was looking back at me. A look that suggested she was broken on the inside as much as her physical body was on the outside. Her mouth moved, then her bottom lip trembled again, and then her head was back against her knee, shaking.

"That's it for now. Time for us to be moving along. Should I send a car to come and get you? Take you to a hotel? There are some lovely ones overlooking the river," said Martin.

His team had all but finished the initial clean-up and were standing around the trolleyed refrigerator that now contained Jay's body. Some of the team were smoking, others just looked bored.

"No. We'll stay here. I owe it to Csaba to put on a brave face tomorrow morning. He doesn't deserve what happened here."

"You are a good person, better than I expected. May you be remembered if that is your want, or forgotten if that is your destiny," said Martin, not flinching at the cheesiness of his farewell while he bowed slightly.

"Tell Csaba that another team will be in contact with him and that if he has any other apartments that need seeing to he can add them to the job requirements."

I nodded.

"Also, if ever you find yourself in Camden, I am always willing to take coffee with old friends."

I nodded again, and took his proffered hand and shook it lightly.

Then he was gone.

*****

"I never meant…," she began.

"Not now," I whispered.

I helped her up and into the bathroom, removed her clothes and lifted her into the shower. I stripped to my underwear and got in, gently washing her scarred, broken, and battered body, rinsing away the shame of her fear.

She cried intermittently while I dried her and a little more as I helped her back into the main room. She sniffed a little as I eased her onto the bed, then curled into a foetal position.

I left her to doze.

The greasy feeling of blood and brain was still on me as I returned to the shower and stood in the steaming stream of water until it began to cool. Every inch of my body lathered in hostel soap, I stood rinsing off in the cool, then frighteningly cold water.

By the time I returned to the bed she was asleep. I crawled in behind her and she moved back toward me, whimpering softly as I tucked into the shape of her knees. She pressed backward, into the hollow of my body, now in full contact with her naked back and buttocks. The hand that I placed over her fell naturally against her breast as I pulled her even closer, with no intent other than to be as close to her as I could be.

# Epilogue.

That was a long time ago now.

We stayed in Budapest until Belinda had healed and then we went home.

I tried to get past the fact that Belinda had been instrumental in Her death, and managed quite successfully. Belinda, on the other hand, could not let it go. It had cut her more violently than she had ever cut herself.

So 'it', the issue of Her, hung between us like a fetid corpse. The stench of it became even more concentrated after we returned home to the Motel and knuckled down to find out the last pieces of the puzzle.

Since Budapest, we knew who had actually killed Her, but Jay hadn't been overly forward about who gave the order in the first place so we returned to the bulletin boards and forums to grasp at the last loose and flapping threads.

The information came to us relatively easily in the scheme of things; it was only a matter of a couple of months of snooping and lurking about before some solid information came our way. Far more preferable to the long-term slog we experienced just finding The Cult in the first place. Perhaps Martin had lifted some of the roadblocks in our way, but we couldn't be sure. In time, for whatever reason, we had all the information we needed.

She was ordered killed by Her father, although not enough proof could be produced to form any kind of legal case. Nonetheless, all the paths we trod in our search lead directly back to him.

Her Father and I didn't have a relationship. He did not approve of his daughter deciding on me as a partner in the giant adventure that is life. I knew that. What I didn't know was the depths of the darkness that had descended upon him after She and I had moved in together.

He had died horribly, succumbing to colon cancer the year before Jay stole into the backyard of the house at The Beach. It seems his passing, and the mailing of documents left in his will, sealed the fate of his daughter. He had begun the project years before his death, had stacked the dominos in their intricate pattern, ready for the simple push of the first tile to set everything in motion. The impetus for that first push was also the last of the actions requested in his will. A letter to a Cult operative, the information then passed to Jay. He couldn't bear to deal with the murder of his child in life, but was more than comfortable with a bullet in Her head after he had died.

Why he didn't choose to simply have me murdered at the same time is open to conjecture, our best guess was that he wanted me to live through it and that he naïvely believed I would ultimately forget Her and move on. For him, it was a simple victory. What he didn't count on was love. True, honest, pure, love. A concept that eluded him entirely.

We found many references to his involvement in facets of The Cult. When overlaying the beliefs and tenets of the factions he was most interested in, it seemed that he simply believed that he could take his daughter into the afterlife, perhaps to start again.

As always, he treated her as a possession until the very last.

I thought of that, of Her being his possession, as the lesser of the evils that hovered around this vile plan. The greater? He simply used the connections to The Cult to resolve something hideous and broken within him. He wanted to be right, and to be right she would have to die, and I would need to be punished.

In truth, I think he was a sad, sick and twisted man who couldn't bear to see two people in love. The idea that we lived together was obviously the final straw.

\*\*\*\*\*

Once we had rounded that out, Belinda and I came to an impasse. I loved her, but not in any sense that would work in the long run. Although we had cut the corpse down from it's fraying noose, the stink of it was still there.

Having nothing to research or work solidly at left a gaping hole in my schedule. A vortex that darkened every time Bam and I came together, an act we did often, playing at being the same as we were before Jay, and Europe.

It couldn't ever be the same. I think we both knew that.

So, I left and travelled. Staying only briefly in backpackers quarters or camping out in a tent if I could find a place suitable to do so. Returning to

Bam's Motel when I was in town, where again we would try to replicate the time before the truth got in the way. All that happened, all that we could agree on without articulating as such was that the floor became less comfortable and the caresses more habitual than passionate.

Months and years passed in this fashion, and I found that I returned to the Motel less and less. Initially a season would pass before I found myself there, then two or three seasons would slip by...

...then a year.

*****

Belinda's father finally succumbed to age, and died. He was in his seventies, but apparently still living in 1965 until the very end.

Belinda took her own life soon after.

She was done with it.

Life.

Her head.

Done.

I got the email while at a guest house in Nepal. On an ancient computer whose screen was deformed at one side from being knocked one too many times off the flimsy bench on which it rested, possibly due to the mad dash that ensued every time it began to rain. Whoever got to it first would throw a garbage bag over it, as the computer's only other protection from the weather was a light matchstick roller blind that had long ago lost it's 'roller' functionality.

*Hi,*

*This is a shitty way of informing you of my demise, although I suspect you won't be at all surprised.*

*I hope you are at least a little sad, though. The only part of this that I don't like is that I'll never see you again. Or share pizza and cheap wine in front of bad TV.*

*I have said it before, and now for the very last time and at my 11th hour, here it is again: I am so sorry about Her. So dreadfully sorry.*

*Please know that I love you, I'm already missing us terribly. It hasn't been the same since Budapest – but really, that's to be expected. The fact that you tried at all to comfort me is a miracle.*

*To me, at least.*

*That said, my actions that will take place shortly are entirely about me. I'm tired, I am sick, and I am done. I had a responsibility to my father, and now he is gone I am free.*

*This is not your fault.*

*With love, truly.*

*B xx*

Tears dropped on the keyboard.

Thousands of messages had been typed from this hostel to loved ones on various continents. Many had sat and leaned over the same damaged machine, squinting to make out all the characters just as I was doing. News from home, babies born, loved ones telling of how much they missed each other.

I hope that none of the messages made their recipients cry as I did. The hostel owner quietly placed a beer on the table beside me and a lit cigarette in an ashtray next to the beer. He laid his hand on my shoulder and whispered a small prayer before leaving me alone in the common room of my tiny Nepalese backpacker retreat.

*****

Belinda left me everything including the Motel and a modest bank account.

I had no desire to enter the Motel business, so I sold it.

The house at The Beach still hadn't sold, and, having no desire to go back, I reduced the price to well below market value. Even so, the first offer to buy it came from someone who was obviously aware that the current owner wanted out, fast. He offered a third less than the asking price.

I took it.

My old apartment was easy to sell, so easy in fact that I couldn't quite believe I hadn't ditched it before. I think I had kept it for so long simply because we, She and I, had been happy there. In some way, I had made it into a shrine to Us. The kind of shrine I had no need to visit, it could have been on the top of a mountain in Sri Lanka for all I cared. Just knowing that there were still objects there that She had placed had hallowed the space.

All of those things would be swept away once the new owners acquired the keys. All the properties were sold including all of their contents, leaving the new occupiers free to do with them what they wished.

The beach house guy contacted me via the selling agent with a message that sounded like he was trying to relieve his guilt after swooping in like carrion foul to peck at the corpse of the house. He asked whether I was sure that I didn't require any of the stuff in the place. "It's not expensive stuff, but there seems to be a few items that look too personal to leave," he had written.

I replied that I didn't want any of it, and if he felt the need to do some good he should call the sporting club to come and take what they needed for their club rooms and various share houses that the young folk invariably rented, desperate to gain their independence from parents. The share houses and surfer's sheds were often filled with such flotsam as could be scavenged from the beach house.

I spent many years travelling, moving from place to place – essentially existing as a moneyed homeless person. I hiked a lot and learned to be more remote, both in personal contact and in physical space. Primarily so when my time came to move on, to leave this world, I would survive long enough to travel under my own power to be as far away as I could be.

Realising that there was a chance that unplanned illness and age might creep up on me, I found myself a space on a Cult monastic collective. Twenty acres of private land bordering a state forest, just for me. All my neighbours (none of whom I have ever seen) respected the privacy of those around them.

I heard that Martin had died. The cause? Old age, apparently, or so the forums I infrequently viewed said. I am prepared to believe them too. Martin had prepared for his departure in a manner that was the opposite of my plan. He wished to be remembered.

I did not.

At that point, the time of Martin's death, the laptop that still bore Belinda's tunnelling software had somehow managed to stay with me, but it was old.

Even now, surprisingly, it has functioned right up to the last, furnishing me with what little information I require. It has lost some keys, and the screen is not so dissimilar to that of the screen that delivered me the news of Belinda's demise, but it works. Power is the bigger issue; the solar panels I fitted to my hideaway have had much more important work over the years than allowing the little computer to work in an on-demand manner.

Sure, it is on its last legs, so to speak, but it has served well and has been – and done – enough. Enough to keep me connected with the goings on of the world, but not enough for me to interact with it. A situation that suited both me, and the machine, admirably.

*****

The years have slid by and I've done all I can to prepare for the next big adventure. The spot I've picked out is about five days hike north of here, remote and truly breathtaking. I've been heading out to it for the last decade or so, making sure that all will be ready for my departure.

What is to prepare? Not much in the scheme of things, but even so I have spent much time in preparation. The earth, too, is a living thing, and I was asking a lot of it – requesting it to take my body in, to hold it as the creatures of the earth come and liquefy my flesh and entrails. Then of course there is the eternal favour: I have asked it to keep my bones hidden for all time.

I've made peace with that patch and I think we trust each other.

I've waited long enough. She has been erased as best as I can tell; all files altered or destroyed. Her name hasn't been Hers for the best part of a quarter of a century now, and my name not far less than that.

And now it is time.

I will soon walk into the forest, then hike the five days north to my plot. Remote and quiet, and beautiful, it's the kind of place that She would like, and I truly hope that I meet her there, waiting in the half light of the trees. I also hope that I have done enough so that we can leave.

Forgotten, we can join hands again and set off on the journey together, the smell of the earth and leaves combined, and the smell of us in the sun, together again, if only for an instant.

Erasure.

Also by A.T.H. Webber

*Broken*

## Acknowledgments

Firstly, thanks to YOU, the reader. You took a chance, and bought a book – probably only after a brief recommendation online, or a gentle nudge from a friend. You took the time to track down, buy, and, if you are reading this, read page after page of my words.

I find the process a truly humbling experience.

Thanks also…

Kim Booker for challenging me to write a full-length novel (some might say fooling me into it).

The draft readers: Julie Talbot, Kam Gillar, Shaun Murphy, Rachel Butler-Russell.

First round of editorial masochism: Lisa Reinisch

Lastly: the biggest "Thank you" of them all goes to my wife and best friend, Karma Auden, for supporting me in all my endeavours no matter how crazy they might sound, and for so many other reasons.

A.T.H. Webber.

June 1st, 2012

www.athwebber.com
www.facebook.com/webberATH

**About the author:**

In 2016, *Erasure* was one of the prize winning entries in the "Montegrappa Writing Prize" – the main award event at the Dubai Festival of Literature.

At the time of Erasure's publication, he and his wife lived in Abu Dhabi, sharing their home with two cats and a dog. They might still be there now.

25012387R00149

Printed in Great Britain
by Amazon